A TOWN CALLED DEFIANCE

Nearly twenty years after the end of the Civil War, one small town near the Mexican border was still strongly Confederate. The locals called their town Defiance and clung to old loyalties. And then a stranger arrived. He saw or heard something that stirred his memory of the past and asked one too many questions. That started the shooting . . . A federal marshal arrived on the scene, but there would be more deadly gunfire before the mystery could be solved.

TOM BENSON

A TOWN CALLED DEFIANCE

Complete and Unabridged

LINFORD
Leicester

First published in Great Britain in 2006 by
Robert Hale Limited
London

First Linford Edition
published 2007
by arrangement with
Robert Hale Limited
London

British Library CIP Data

Benson, Tom, *1929* –
    A town called Defiance.—Large print ed.—
Linford western library
1. Western stories
2. Large type books
I. Title
823.9'14 [F]

ISBN 978–1–84617–735–4

Published by
F. A. Thorpe (Publishing)
Anstey, Leicestershire

Set by Words & Graphics Ltd.
Anstey, Leicestershire
Printed and bound in Great Britain by
T. J. International Ltd., Padstow, Cornwall

This book is printed on acid-free paper

The large freight wagon was drawn by six mules. Two more brought up the rear as reserves for the heavy load that came into town every few weeks from the railhead. The driver and his guard were sweating in the fierce heat of noon. It trickled down their faces and made thin paths amid the dust. They were large men, unshaven for days and with heavy moustaches that were greying and tobacco-stained.

Defiance was a small town with one main street, a regular Wells Fargo staging-post, and a newly installed telegraph that was still a novelty to the children. They looked in at the windows of the office until chased away by a furious clerk. It was a prosperous place, aided by cattle ranches all around and by nearby hills which were yielding copper that brought workers into the area. Timber felling had also started and there was talk of a railroad.

Defiance was also a fiercely southern town. And Southern in the political sense. It had been virtually founded by families forced from their homes as the war overtook them. They settled in a remote part that was as far away as possible from the evils of a Yankee victory. Defiance was well named, and so was the Southern Star saloon, and the Beauregard Hotel on the main street.

Marshal Smith watched the freight wagon as it drew up at each store that was expecting a delivery from the big cities. The driver and his mate carried in the various loads while the lawman lounged happily on the shaded stoop of the jailhouse.

Matt Smith liked watching other people work. It made him stand out as a man in a privileged position. His cousin was the mayor and he had his younger brother as deputy. It was a neatly sewn-up situation and he revelled in it. Matt was a big man in his forties. His face was blotchy and his scant hair was brushed forward in a greyish mass. He chewed tobacco as he watched the wagon and the folk passing by on the street. After a glance at the angle of the sun he decided that it was time for a meal. He dragged his bulk from the chair and crossed the street towards the Southern Star. A plate of ham and a few drinks would be waiting for him there.

He nodded to the wagon driver as he passed and just caught some of the conversation between him and the other wagoner. The marshal's head went up as though some alarm bell had rung. He turned back and grabbed the elbow of the driver's assistant.

'Where you from, fella?' he asked roughly.

The man was as big as the marshal but older and with a paunch that hung over his belt. He eyed the aggressor without fear and pulled his arm away as he looked the marshal straight in the eye.

'What's it to you?' he asked without respect for the lawman's badge. 'I don't take kindly to bein' pushed around when I'm doin' no harm to nobody.'

'You got an accent that folk in these parts wouldn't like to hear,' Marshal Smith said grimly. 'You ain't carryin' a gun and this town is full of Southern folk who don't like to have Yankees struttin' around on their patch.'

The other wagoner put down the cask he was carrying.

'This is Will Rooney, Marshal,' he said quietly. 'Don't worry about him keepin' his voice down. He knows the feelin' round these parts.'

'Where's old Steve?' the lawman asked.

'Laid off with some sorta lung trouble. The doc reckons he won't work no more. Will is usually on the eastern route but I'm sure as hell glad to have someone with me who can pull his weight. Old Steve was gettin' past it.'

Matt Smith looked up and down the street.

'Well, just keep your voice down, fella,' he said. 'And don't get into no trouble. This is a Southern town, remember.'

'I can't understand this,' Will Rooney said in a genuinely puzzled voice. 'The war's been over nigh on eighteen years. Can't folk let the past be forgot?'

Matt Smith looked at him and the lawman's eyes showed a certain compassion for the man's innocence.

'The folks that pioneered this town was all run outa their own spreads by the Yankees,' he explained tautly. 'Lost everything, they did, and moved south towards the border. This was a real one-horse place when they arrived here. They built it up and others joined them. Like callin' on like, as you might say. Folks here have known real suffering, so forgivin' don't come easy to them. This is as far from them crooked politicos in Washington as they can get. And it still ain't far enough. A Yankee accent ain't a way of makin' friends in this neck of the woods. So

5

just you remember that, fella.'

The man nodded.

'I won't do nothin' to offend, Marshal,' he said with a new friendliness. 'I served in the war myself, and I got my own bad memories too.'

The marshal nodded and went into the saloon while the two men finished their round of the stores before going to unhitch the mules and feed them. Then they tended to their own needs for the night.

The freight company paid the men a small amount to take up board and lodgings in the towns they visited. Being old-timers and used to roughing it, they nearly always camped in the freight wagon and spent the lodging-money in the local saloons.

Tonight was no exception. After a quick bite to eat and a wash under the nearest water-pump, they strolled in comfortable companionship down the main street in the cool of the evening and took their places at the bar of the Southern Star. It was a cheerful refuge, adorned with large gilt mirrors that reflected the light from the many brass and copper oil-lamps. These were newly lit and there was still a vague smell from them that lingered in the air.

'Keep your voice low in here, Will,' Ted Laurie reminded his companion. 'These folks is real touchy.'

'I'll watch it,' the other man promised. 'But this is one hell of a town. Can't they forget the blamed war? I'm sure as hell tryin' to.'

'I guess not. They all suffered too much, I reckon.'

The two men drank quietly as the saloon began to fill up and a couple of card-schools got busy in a far corner. There was a little group of well-dressed men at the far end of the bar. Their cigar smoke curled up to the stained ceiling as they talked and drank imported whiskey. Their voices were loud and full of confidence. The Southern accents were clear to all who listened.

Will Rooney kept his voice down. He

looked around with interest and enjoyed the decent beer that spoke of the superior class of trade that the saloon catered for. As the evening wore on he mellowed towards the other drinkers and viewed the motley crowd with less hostility. Then something caught his eye. His face took on a remote look as he stared unbelievingly across the room.

'What's the matter, Will?'

The words jolted him back to reality and he swallowed his drink from a glass that trembled in his hand.

'Oh, just had a thought from the past,' he muttered. 'Do you know these folks, Ted?'

'Only the storekeepers. Why?'

'I was just wondering. Some of them look real prosperous, that's all.'

Ted Laurie nodded. 'Well, it's a busy town,' he said, 'and gettin' bigger every time I come here. There's sure one hell of a lotta money in Defiance.'

Will Rooney nodded silent agreement and bought more beer. The bar began to empty as the evening drew to a close. There were a small number of noisy drunks, but Marshal Smith was present and nobody felt like causing trouble. Ted Laurie was deep in conversation and did not notice that Will had vanished. His companion had left to follow a group of men who were on their way home after a convivial night out. His face was set grimly as he trailed one of them with a fierce determination.

Ted Laurie eventually left the saloon himself and headed back for the welcoming freight wagon and his bed. He expected to find Will Rooney already there, but his blankets were still rolled up. The driver settled himself down, put out the stub of candle, and went to sleep.

Ted was not quite sure what woke him, but he lay there in a slightly drunken state trying to puzzle it out. He wondered what the noise was in the darkness beyond the corrals. He could hear one or two shouts and some activity from the nervous mules and horses. A few flickering lights threw shadows on the canvas of the wagon and Ted Laurie decided to get up and see what was happening.

There was a gathering crowd at the near end of the main street. He cut through an alley and went over to join them. He could catch a glimpse of a man who lay on the ground with blood pouring from a chest wound. The marshal was pushing his way through and his deputy was already there with a gun in his hand.

'Carry him to Doc Mason's place,' the marshal ordered some of the heftier men. 'And be mighty careful with the fella. He's lookin' to be in a bad state.'

Ted Laurie noticed the .44 Colt that lay on the ground by the wounded man's right hand. As the helpers moved in to lift the body, he also recognized the fallen man. It was Will Rooney.

Marshal Smith stood and watched the crowd moving off towards the doctor's office. He looked at his brother, the deputy, and then took him by the arm to steer him towards the jailhouse.

'We need to talk about this, Larry,' he said in a quiet voice. 'You got some explainin' to do.'

Larry Smith holstered his gun, picked up the other weapon, and accompanied the marshal across the street to their office. The light was on and the two men sat down on either side of the desk. Larry was a taller and slimmer version of his elder brother. He had a hard, firm mouth and deep-set eyes under dark brows. Marshal Smith took a whiskey bottle from a drawer and poured them both a drink.

'So what was it all about?' he asked.

'Well, I was just patrollin' the far end of town when this fella comes out of the alley by the baker's store. He's wavin' his arms all over and shoutin' somethin' about folks round here bein' a bunch of no-good skunks. He was real drunk and lookin' to make trouble. I went over and told him to quieten it, but he just got mad and drew on me. I was lucky to get off a shot. He was one real mean son of a bitch.'

Marshal Smith studied his brother's face carefully. The lawman was fair-minded and he had an uneasy feeling about the story. 'What about his accent?' he asked casually.

'Accent?' Larry Smith looked puzzled.

'Yeah. If the fella was makin' so much noise, you must surely have noticed what part of the South he hailed from. Was he local, or Texan, or maybe a Virginian come a-callin' on us?'

'Oh, yeah, I see what you mean, Matt. Well, I reckoned him for one of them wild Texans we hear so much about. Them fellas got no respect for law and order.'

'And no more have you, Larry,' the marshal said grimly. 'That fella was from the North. He was an old army man, and I'd already told him to keep his mouth shut and to behave himself in my town. And he didn't draw no gun on you.'

Larry Smith flushed angrily and jumped up from the chair. His whiskey glass went flying and his voice was choking and furious when he spoke.

'He sure as hell did!' he yelled. 'Do you think I'd go shootin' an unarmed man?'

'Anybody see him draw on you?'

There was a slight pause.

'Well, I reckon not. But I ain't bein' called a liar. Not even by my own brother.'

'Your brother ain't callin' you a liar, Larry. The marshal of this town is callin' you a liar. Now, I'll tell you somethin', fella. He weren't carryin' no gun. And that .44 was lyin' near his right hand. I ain't no baby-faced rube not to have noticed that he was left-handed when he was unloadin' that wagon earlier today.'

2

Will Rooney was carried gently to the doctor's office where Mrs Mason already had the door opened to steer them into the surgery where they placed the man on a padded table.

'Wally ain't here, I'm afraid,' she said as she turned up the oil lamps. 'He's out deliverin' Mrs Bluitt's latest. They always have to wait until it's nigh on sleepin' time before they decide to call out the doctor. If this fella's bad hurt, I figure as all I can do is to stop the bleedin' and stitch him up.'

A small man pushed his way between the hefty bearers of the injured freighter. He was stooped and middle-aged, with gold-rimmed glasses and a nearly bald pate that shone under the lights. Ralph Loman was manager of the Beauregard Hotel and his neat dress and prissy, old-maidish manner made him the butt of local humour.

'I can manage,' he said in a commanding voice they had never heard from him before. 'Is there a surgical kit available?'

Emma Mason nodded dumbly and went to open a cupboard. One of the other men pushed the little manager in the back.

'When did you take up doctorin' then?' he asked with a grin and wink at his mates.

'I was a field-hospital orderly durin' the war,' Ralph Loman said proudly. 'I've tended many a wounded man while you was still in the schoolhouse. Now, get out of here and let Mrs Mason and me do our work.'

The men retreated obediently and the doctor's wife aided the hotel manager to work on the wound. He shook his head sadly as he peered through his spectacles. The damage was serious and not even a professional surgeon could hope to do much for the man. Ralph Loman was able to stanch the bleeding and was covering the wound when Will Rooney opened his eyes for the first time. He had been groaning slightly from the moment he was hit, but now he fell silent. His eyes blinked as he stared up at the copper oil-lamp. He turned his head slightly to look at the man who leaned over him.

There was a trickle of blood from his mouth and he coughed slightly. Mrs Mason picked up the swabs and left the surgery to dispose of them.

'Just rest quietly, fella,' Ralph Loman said soothingly. 'It's all finished now. The worst is over and the wound's closed. You just need to sleep. I'll give you somethin' for the pain.'

Will Rooney's eyes suddenly seemed to brighten.

'It *was* him,' he said softly. 'I knew I couldn't be wrong. It *was* Sergeant Bedser.'

'What was that about?' Mrs Mason asked as she came back to the surgery.

'Just rambling,' the hotel manager told her in a slightly puzzled voice. 'Has the doc left any morphine?'

She shook her head. 'All I got here is chloroform and a little ether.'

She crossed to look at the injured man. He had closed his eyes and appeared to be unconscious again.

'Did you take the bullet out?' she asked.

Ralph Loman shook his head. He steered her away from the table.

'Too far gone,' he whispered. 'It's pierced the lung and lodged in his spine. He ain't got long to go. I thought morphine might help, but he don't seem to be in pain.'

'We'll let him sleep,' she agreed. 'I've got some laudanum if he needs it. Thanks for your help, Mr Loman. There weren't nothin' much I could have done. Bein' a midwife is about my limit. The marshal's here, by the way. Wants to know what's goin' on.'

Ralph Loman washed his hands. He looked in despair at the stains on his waistcoat, and then went to meet the lawman. Matt Smith stood in the middle of the living-room with a coffee-pot in his hand. He poured out a cup for the hotel manager and pointed to the articles on the table.

'Strange sorta fella for a town like this,' he said softly. 'Discharge papers from one of them Massachusetts volunteer regiments; a real cheap watch, and fifty new one-dollar bills. Now where the hell would he get that sorta money?'

Mrs Mason joined them, wiping her hands on a bloodstained towel.

'He's gone,' she said sorrowfully. 'We did all we could but that brother of your'n was a good shot, Matt. Too good.'

She looked at the man's few belongings and then poured herself some coffee.

'One of them things what happens when a fella gets drunk and shoots his mouth off,' the lawman said. 'Larry reckons that he got real wild back there.'

The marshal spoke with no great

conviction. He poked among the other few items on the table.

'I see there's an address here,' he said. 'Back in Phoenix. That's one hell of a way from Defiance. I'll ask Ted Laurie if he knows anythin' more about him. I suppose I gotta let his folks know he's dead.'

Ted Laurie had stayed at the back of the crowd during all the excitement. He was not too keen to be associated with his fellow freighter if there was trouble. Ted knew the temper of the Southern town and he just watched quietly as the injured man was carried into the surgery followed by the hotel manager and the marshal. He had noticed the marshal go to the jailhouse first with his deputy. He looked pretty angry when he emerged and ignored folk around him as he made for the doctor's house.

It was an hour or so later when Marshal Smith came to the freight wagon where Ted was trying to sleep. He woke him by banging on the tailboard. Matt Smith told him of Will

Rooney's death and asked about any family he might have.

Ted shook his head a little sadly. 'There ain't no wife, she died a few years back,' he said. 'But there's a son got a hog-breedin' farm near Phoenix. Will used to speak about him now and then. Hoped to retire there, I reckon. Said hogs were friendlier than people.'

Ted Laurie turned up the little lamp that hung from the centre beam of the wagon. He could see the marshal's face better now.

'He didn't have no gun, Marshal,' he said. 'Told me he'd had enough of guns in the war.'

'Must have picked it up somewheres. What will you do now?'

Ted shrugged. 'Well, I reckon as how I'll have to send a message back to the depot, and then carry on as best I can. There's only two more towns to visit. Then I pick up some more freight and head for home. Will you be writin' to his son?'

'I guess so.' The marshal turned to go

and then hesitated for a moment.

'How much money do you reckon he had on him?' he asked.

'Money? Hell, he'd be lucky to have five dollars in his breeches. Why d'you ask?'

'Did he know anybody here in town?'

'No. Said he'd never been here before. Why?'

'I was just curious. Us lawmen is like that.'

The marshal strode away and Ted Laurie sat in the back of the wagon with a puzzled look on his face. Whatever he thought, he knew that in a town like Defiance, it was best not to open his mouth.

The marshal's brother was at the jailhouse. He looked a little uneasy as Matt Smith flung down the dead man's belongings on the desk.

'Where exactly was this fella when you first clapped eyes on him?' the marshal asked tersely.

'He was comin' outa that alley next to the baker's store. Roarin' and bawlin' somethin' awful, he was.'

'Never mind that, Larry. Just stick with the truth. Where had he come from?'

'How the hell would I know? He was just there.'

'Was there a light in the store?'

'No. Not at that time of night. Why are you askin' these questions, Matt? I was just doin' my job.'

'Yeah, but who for? Somebody sent you after that fella. Told you to make sure he got shot.'

Larry shrugged. He suddenly felt that he was on safer ground. 'Hell, Matt, we both know what folks give the orders in this town. I just happened to be on the spot. It could have been you.'

'I wouldn't have murdered the man, fella. Not even for Defiance.'

'It wasn't murder!'

'Like hell it wasn't. Look at this. Fifty dollars in the pocket of a freight-hauler who's lucky if he gets eight dollars a week. Now, I ain't askin' no more questions. But don't ever try foolin' me again. You and me is kin, and we gotta be straight with each other.'

There was a knock at the door before Larry could answer, and when it opened, Ralph Loman sidled into the office.

'I thought I'd just look in, Marshal,' he said in his unctuous voice. 'You'll be writin' to this fella's family, and I know what a distressin' job it can be. I thought I could perhaps be of service. Clerkin' is all part of my business, and writin' letters is a bit of a chore for a man of action like yourself.'

The lawman breathed an almost audible sigh of relief.

'You sure as hell got the right of it there,' he said with a grin. 'I'd be real obliged if you'd let this son of his know what happened. Tell him that the town will see his pa gets a good funeral and that we'll be sendin' his belongings through the Wells Fargo office.'

They discussed the matter for a few more minutes before the hotel manager left. He took with him all the paperwork he needed. And the most important bit of that was the document showing Will Rooney's service and discharge from the Union army.

★ ★ ★

Ralph Loman sent more than one letter off and then had to wait impatiently for some answers. Will Rooney was buried quietly, Matt Smith and his brother were a bit distant from each other for a time, but things gradually got back to normal.

The eagerly awaited letter finally arrived. Over two months had passed and Ralph Loman had almost given up hoping. He retired to his comfortable office behind the reception desk and read it several times with increasing delight. Then he hid it away and pondered his next move. Ralph Loman was a cautious man.

He was so preoccupied that he took little notice of one of his latest guests. Hank Donovan was a large and florid man with a round, smiling face and greying hair. He was neatly dressed; he carried a single gun and was more like a townsman than some country rube. His voice was rich and friendly. He drank at the Southern Star and his accent made him an acceptable part of the community.

If asked his business, he mentioned some vague interest in copper-mining, and bought drinks freely enough to stem further enquiries. He rode out of town now and then on a rented horse, and soon became part of the general scene.

There was also another man in town who passed without any comment. He was younger and his dark face was permanently set in a hard scowl that deterred questions of any sort. He looked like a cowpoke, came in on a grey gelding that was getting on in years, and he carried a gun at his side. He stayed at Ma Blanes boarding-house, paid the rent regularly, and bothered nobody.

He often drank at the Southern Star and watched what went on around him. He also picked up the local gossip but the sullen expression never changed as he listened to people talking. The marshal and his deputy looked him over once or twice, but the young fellow never got drunk or made trouble.

Ralph Loman was in a thoughtful world of his own. His hand trembled as he wrote two more letters. He sealed them carefully and then took one along to his bank. Having delivered that, he left the other one with his lawyer before going back to the hotel and pouring a stiff shot of whiskey.

He had taken all the precautions he could and was now aiming to be a rich and important man in the town of Defiance.

3

The town was drying off after the heavy seasonal rain. Steam rose from the main street as the freight wagon arrived with Ted Laurie's hand on the reins. He had a new assistant now: a young fellow with fair hair and a wide, childish face. They got down and started to unload at the hardware store.

Marshal Smith waved a hand in greeting as he caught Ted Laurie's eye. The lawman was in his usual position on the jailhouse stoop and the best part of three months had gone by since the shooting. Defiance was a quiet place and the whole episode was forgotten. The wagon moved on to the gun-store and stopped again. Nobody seemed to take much notice, but one man was watching through the window of the saloon.

It was the young fellow with the

sullen glower. He stood with a beer in his grasp as he viewed the street. His facial expression seemed to lighten a little when the wagon appeared. He swallowed the warm drink and wiped his mouth with a rough hand.

Ted Laurie went through his usual routine and ended the day by making camp in the wagon behind the spread of corrals. He rinsed off his face before setting out for an evening at the Southern Star. His young helper went off to a more exciting saloon where the rooms above were rented to young women. A piano played there all night and nobody cared that the drinks were watered down as the patrons got more intoxicated.

The Southern Star was different. It was the place for the more respectable elements and Ted Laurie felt comfortable there. He leaned on the bar, nodded to the few people he knew, and quietly enjoyed his drink. He hardly noticed the dark-faced young man who stood on his right.

'I reckon you must be Ted Laurie,' the man said in a neutral sort of voice. 'I've heard tell of you.'

'Is that a fact?' The freight driver looked at the young fellow properly for the first time. 'I've been haulin' freight to this town for nigh on fifteen years.'

'Yeah. And once with my pa. I'm Jason Rooney.'

Ted put down his glass and reached out a hand to the young man. They shook firmly and Jason Rooney almost managed a smile.

'I'm sure sorry about your pa,' Ted said with feeling. 'Him and me got on well together and his shootin' has sure preyed on my mind ever since. Should never have happened.'

'That's what I reckon too. Tell me what it was all about?'

'Didn't the marshal write you?'

'Oh, sure. Just said that there's been a drunken shoot-out and that my pa had been buried all right and proper. Even sent me his belongings and some cash money.'

Ted nodded. 'Yeah. I'd like to have written myself but readin' and figurin' ain't quite my style. I can't find no sense in how your pa died, and that's a fact.'

He told of the events in the town that night and how the gun had lain beside the fallen man.

'It were all wrong,' he said firmly. 'Your pa had no gun and he was left-handed. Even the marshal spotted that. But his deputy claimed your pa drew first. That was the end of it.'

'Well, it sure wasn't Pa's gun they sent me, and I can't figure where all that money came from.'

'All that money?' It was the first that Ted had heard of a large sum of money.

'I didn't hear tell of no money,' he said. 'Your pa was like me, with a few dollars in his pocket, and no more. Where in hell would he get money?'

'That's what has me beat, Mr Laurie. The marshal sent me thirty-one dollars and a few cents. Said they was found on Pa. The mortician had already been paid out of that cash. I reckon that means there must have been fifty dollars or more to start with. That just don't seem possible.'

Ted Laurie shook his head in bewilderment. 'I'm with you on that, lad,' he said. 'Unless your pa went gamblin' when he left the saloon. But I don't reckon so. He weren't no gamblin' fella that I could tell. And he weren't gone long enough.'

'Never did play cards. Never had the money for it,' Jason Rooney assured him.

Ted Laurie recalled the question Marshal Smith had asked him. He told the young man of the lawman's enquiry about Will Rooney knowing anybody in town. Jason shook his head.

'Never knew nobody in this part of the world,' he said slowly. 'Unless it was some fella from the past. Maybe somebody he knew durin' the war.'

The two men drank in silence for a few minutes. Then Jason Rooney put down his glass.

'Pa weren't no fightin' fella,' he said quietly. 'He always told me and Ma that he'd had enough of that to last him a lifetime. And he weren't no trouble-makin' drunk neither. I reckon this deputy marshal they got here killed him for some reason we don't know about.'

Ted Laurie looked around uneasily. The saloon was filling up and it made him nervous.

'Lookit, Jason,' he said quietly, 'this town is all Southern pride and a-worshippin' of Jeff Davis and all them fellas. You and me just don't fit. The marshal is a cousin of the mayor and the deputy is the marshal's younger brother. I'm inclined to agree with you, but I intend to get outa here with a whole hide. I don't aim to be no Pinkerton fella, pokin' my nose into local politics. If I was you, I'd go home and forget about it. They don't call this place Defiance for nothing.'

'I aim to make 'em pay for my father, Mr Laurie.' The young man's voice was harsh now and a little too loud. One or two heads turned in their direction and Ted Laurie wished himself elsewhere.

'Keep your voice down,' he muttered. 'The marshal's at the far end of the bar.'

Jason Rooney glanced across and then turned back to Ted Laurie.

'So where will his deputy be?' he asked.

'In the jailhouse or on patrol, I should imagine. You ain't gonna go causin' trouble, Jason? This is one dangerous place.'

He got no answer and had to stand watching the young man leave the saloon. Ted Laurie was undecided for a moment and then moved towards the door himself. He reckoned that the best move was for him to go back to the freight wagon and settle down for the night. Trouble was the last thing he needed.

The jailhouse was lit by a single oil-lamp from the ceiling. The place was warm and Deputy Marshal Larry Smith was dozing in a chair by the stove. An enamel coffee-pot was grumbling away and a few moths circled the lamp and threw moving shadows across the room.

The lawman woke with a start when the door opened and then crashed noisily shut. He turned to face a young man who had been around town for the last week or so. The stranger stood, his back to the door and with one hand near the .44 at his side. The deputy marshal scrambled to his feet, his chair squeaking on the boards as it was pushed aside.

'What the hell do you want, fella?' Larry Smith bawled.

'I want the man who shot my pa.'

The voice was low but there was a menace that stopped the lawman in his tracks.

'What in hell are you talkin' about?' he asked. 'Who's been shot? I didn't hear nothin' goin' on out there.'

'I'm talkin' about Will Rooney. You shot him down in the street a few months back. Then you claimed he was carryin' a gun. I'm callin' you one lyin' son of a bitch. You'd better draw, fella.'

Larry Smith hesitated for a moment. He had only just woken up and the words were not sinking in properly.

'Look, fella, I just did my job,' he stammered. 'He was roarin' drunk and shoutin' all over town. When I tried to stop him, he just drew on me. That's all there was to it. I'm sorry it was your pa, but I gotta keep law and order around here. Now go home and don't make trouble in a place where Yankees ain't exactly popular.'

'I told you to draw.'

The words were harsh and chilling in the warmth of the office. Larry Smith backed away a couple of feet as his hand slid down for the butt of the Colt.

The door flew open at that moment and Jason Rooney was struck in the back by the force of it. He stumbled forward, drawing the gun as he tried to recover his balance. He swung round to try and cover both enemies. He let fly a single shot and heard a yelp of pain from whoever entered the office. But that was about the last thing he ever experienced. Larry Smith fired wildly and a lucky shot caught the young man in the upper chest. He staggered, tried to swing round on the deputy, and then collapsed.

Marshal Smith was leaning against the open door. Blood poured from his left arm and he clutched it in agony. His brother looked down at the dead body and a grin of triumph lit up his face.

'You sure came in at the right time, Matt,' held cheerfully.

'Not for me, I didn't,' the marshal snapped. 'Get me over to Doc Mason's place before I ruin our nice clean floor.' He looked down at the dead man. 'I had a feelin' about him in the saloon, and when I saw him comin' over here, I sure as hell smelt trouble. Now, help get me outa here. My arm's broke.'

A crowd had gathered outside the jailhouse when the two men emerged. The mayor was pushing through to make his presence felt. He was quickly told the details and put his head round the door to look at the body of Jason Rooney.

The mayor did not like the sight of blood and quickly turned to the crowd to tell them how heroic the lawmen had been. Mayor Smith was a small man, inclined to fat and with a belly that housed a large gold watch-chain. His jowls quivered when he talked and his hands gestured to drive any point home.

'Now, folks,' he bawled over the excited noise, 'we just dealt with a Yankee troublemaker here, so you can all go home and be thankful we got some law and order in our town. The marshal's slight hurt but the fella who caused all the fuss is as dead as Abe Lincoln.'

People were peering in at the windows of the jailhouse and one man recognized the body that lay on the floor.

'He was in the Southern Star!' he

shouted. 'He was all go-to-meetin' friendly with that fella what hauls the freight. They're two of a kind. Yankee-lovers!'

People turned to look at each other as they sought the man who had been mentioned. Ted Laurie had been wise to go back to the wagon.

There was a rumble of anger among the crowd and an almost automatic movement towards Ma Blane's boarding-house. That was where most of the poorer visitors stayed. She was standing on the stoop, watching all the excitement. She hurriedly explained that the freight-haulers saved money by sleeping in their wagon.

The mob was getting larger and noisier as it moved towards the corrals behind the main street. A rope was produced from somewhere, and the mayor made a half-hearted attempt to intervene. Nobody took any notice of him and he hurried to the doctor's house where the front door stood open. Doc Mason was treating the marshal while young Larry Smith watched the operation.

'They're gonna lynch the freight fella,' the mayor panted. 'You gotta stop 'em, Larry.'

The young deputy looked at his cousin with a mixture of fear and defiance.

'I can't stop a mob by myself,' he said bleakly. 'Unless some fella in authority is able to deputize a dozen men or more. Are you gonna do that, Cousin Davy?'

The mayor swallowed noisily. 'You know damned well I can't. They're all in that mob.'

'Then I'm stayin' here, and you'd better do the same.' The marshal nodded his head in sleepy agreement and the doctor paused long enough to concur. Nobody was going to tackle a popular lynching.

Two men were following the mob. The well-dressed stranger strolled along in the footsteps of the crowd, quietly smoking a cigar as he looked on impassively. The manager of the Beauregard Hotel had watched events from the stoop and now joined the townsfolk by instinct as much as anything else. He hated the thought of a hanging but it drew him like a magnet.

He saw them surround the wagon and drag Ted Laurie out of it. The man pushed and shoved as he cried out for help. His voice was drowned by angry shouts as some of the crowd tried to punch and kick him. Ralph Loman looked on in fascinated horror as the blacksmith looped the rope over the man's neck and dragged him to the livery stable. Someone had already gone to the upper floor and flung open the small door that gave on to the loading-beam.

The rope was thrown up, hoisted over the beam, and a score of willing hands dragged on it until Ted Laurie dangled in the air. His legs kicked and his hands flailed as he tried to free the rope. Then his movements suddenly stopped and the crowd let out a cheer.

There was a slight pause as they watched the body sway gently in the warm breeze. A silence fell on the town and Ralph Loman muttered a prayer to a God he seldom thought about. The crowd began to break up. The excitement was over and there was a change in the air. Shame was written on many faces as folk began to move slowly away.

Ralph Loman started to walk back to the hotel. The whole thing had sickened him and he needed a drink. And then he recalled something and his face broke into a secret smile.

4

Major Wallace's daily stroll through town was something to behold. He was a tall and elegant man with a fierce white moustache and sideburns that added grandeur to his finely chiselled face. A black patch covered his left eye and his right hand had two fingers missing. He carried his war wounds proudly despite a slight limp. His frock-coat was a pale fawn, with a suede waistcoat and gold watch-chain. His hat was doffed to the ladies while he waved the malacca cane at his male friends in cheery greeting. He was on his way to the Beauregard Hotel.

He owned it. Major Wallace had bought the rundown place and turned it in to an elegant haven fit for Southerners of discriminating tastes. He had a good manager. Old Ralph Loman was honest and efficient. The place ticked over like a well-kept Eli Woods clock, and the major had a decent income from it.

Ralph Loman was in his office as always at that time of day. The books were in order. There were enough guests to make the management content, and the owner nodded his head in satisfaction as he went through the figures. After a few words of approval and a small glass of whiskey, he stood up to leave.

'Before you go, Major,' Ralph Loman said in his unctuous tones, 'There is somethin' I would like to discuss.'

The ex-military man looked down at the slightly slumped figure behind the desk. There was a certain edginess to the manager's voice.

'Yes, Ralph? I'm always happy to help out with any problem.' The major sat down again.

'Well, I've been workin' for you now these last seventeen years or so,' Ralph said meekly, 'and they've been very happy times. Very happy indeed. But I feel that I've reached a point when I must make a change in my life.'

Major Wallace frowned. He was not accustomed to having disruptions to his routine.

'You're thinking of leaving, Ralph?' he asked in a hurt voice. 'Well, if it's a question of money . . . '

'No, no. Not exactly, Major, but I have plans. I want to own a hotel of my own.'

'Own a hotel? That costs big money, my dear man. A great deal of money. How are you going to manage it?'

'I have the money, Major, and I know which hotel I want. This one.'

There was a long silence while the words ran through the major's mind, to show confusion on his florid face.

'I wasn't figuring on selling,' he said at last. 'And if I did, the price would be a pretty steep one. Nobody knows better than you how good the business is.'

The little man swallowed noisily and put a hand in the pocket of his waist-coat. He took out a five-dollar piece and placed it on the desk between them.

'I have the price right here, Major,'

he said in as calm a voice as he could muster. He watched the changing expressions on the owner's face as the man tried to work things out.

'You do seem to have a touch of the sun, my dear fellow,' Major Wallace eventually said as he stood up to leave. 'I'll put it down to overwork and say no more on the matter. I can get another manager, you know.'

Ralph Loman smiled slyly and held up a restraining hand.

'Don't go, Major,' he said. 'I have a little story to tell you.'

There was something hypnotic in the look the mild little man gave his employer. Major Wallace sat down again and Ralph Loman leaned across the desk.

'You'll recall that the freight wagon came into town a few months back with a new man helpin' Ted Laurie,' he said slowly. 'The new fella had a Yankee accent and he was warned to keep his mouth shut in a town like Defiance. He took a drink in the Southern Star the night they got here. He was dead an hour or so later. He also had money in his pocket that no freight hauler could expect to have.'

The major frowned. 'I don't see the point of all this,' he broke in.

'Be patient, Major. Our brave deputy didn't kill the man outright. He was still alive when I was treatin' his wound. And he told me somethin' real important. He told me why he was killed.'

Major Wallace's face was a slightly paler shade and he sat rigidly in his chair.

'He told me that it was a Sergeant Bedser,' Ralph Loman said with quiet satisfaction. 'Y'know, Major, I couldn't figure that out. There was nobody in town by that name. Then the marshal showed me the fella's Yankee discharge papers. He'd been a sergeant himself in one of them volunteer regiments. So I wrote to a friend of mine up in Washington. Asked him if there had been a Sergeant Bedser in the same regiment as Will Rooney. And do you know what happened?'

He paused with a slight smile on his face. There was no reply as the hotel owner sat as though paralysed in his chair.

'After one hell of a long time, I got back a message to say that there had been a Sergeant Bedser. Wounded in the face and left eye, he was. Lost two fingers on his right hand, and got himself a broken leg in the battle of Shiloh. Then he was given an office job because he could read and write. Ended up as a clerk to the officer in charge of pay. And do you know what Sergeant Bedser did, Major? He killed two other clerks and skipped with the regimental payroll.'

The temperature in the office seemed to have dropped as the two men sat on either side of the desk.

'And you think I'm this Sergeant Bedser?' Major Wallace asked with an attempt at a scornful laugh.

'I certainly do. And Will Rooney recognized you in that saloon because of your wounds. He had fifty dollars on him when he died. And you gave him that to keep his mouth shut. Then you ran off to that deputy marshal, and he killed him for you.'

Major Wallace stood up majestically. He put one finger against the five-dollar coin and pushed it towards Ralph Loman contemptuously. He had recovered his poise and looked every inch the Southern gentleman.

'And you imagine you can scare me with a tale like that?' he asked calmly. 'I'm a powerful man in this town, and all I have to do is to step along to the marshal's office. He'll have you in front of the judge before you know what hit you. You're a very silly man, to end a decent life like this.'

Ralph Loman was not cowed by the words. He leaned back in his chair and stared at the other man.

'There was a lynchin' here the other day, as you might recall,' he said quietly. 'And all because a fella just shared a drink with a Yankee's son. What would the folks do if they found out that Major Wallace deserted from the Bluebelly army with a load of stolen money? Then posed as a Confederate officer and hero and made fools of the whole town?'

Major Wallace's mouth twitched nervously. 'You're on dangerous ground, fella,' he said hoarsely.

'The accent is beginnin' to fall away, Sergeant Bedser,' Ralph mocked him. 'And I'm no freight hauler with a few drinks under his belt. I've written some letters, and they're safe in the hands of folk around town who are real Southerners. They're to be opened if anythin' happens to me. Like it did to Will Rooney. You wouldn't look too good swingin' from the livery stable loadin'-beam, would you?'

Major Wallace sat down again. He placed his hands palms down on the desk and breathed a deep, almost theatrical sigh.

'A man does funny things when he's young,' he said in a low voice. 'I fought for the Union and suffered one hell of a beatin' at Shiloh. Then I'm surrounded by money all of a sudden. It was the sorta money no ordinary fella could ever hope to see. I'd served my time, done my duty, and I felt the bastards owed me. They owed all us young fellas for plungin' us into war while they skulked safely at home. Can you really blame me, Ralph?'

'I can't. So can you blame me?'

There was a slight pause before the former major grinned with an almost boyish pleasure.

'You're right there, fella. We're a couple of rogues,' he chuckled. 'So let's do a deal. I'll make this place over to you and you'll keep your mouth shut. After all, when you really think about it, folk round here would probably lynch you as well. For coverin' up my past. We'd be swingin' on that beam side by side.'

The two men struck a deal and shook hands. There was no sincerity but Major Wallace was at least safe for long enough to work out how to dispose of the man who had once worked for him like some well-drilled lackey.

He left the hotel without acknowledging any of the people he passed. That was why he never noticed one of the guests who sat in the foyer reading a Tombstone newspaper. Hank Donovan watched the retreating figure with interest. He glanced at the closed door of the office and waited patiently. When Ralph Loman emerged a few minutes later, he seemed to carry himself with a new confidence. There was an air of authority in his walk as he smiled at his guest.

'Lovely day, Mr Donovan,' he said cheerfully. 'I hope you're enjoying our little town.'

'I find it very interesting, Mr Loman.'

★   ★   ★

The mayor's office was hot and smoky. Davy Smith presided with a glass of whiskey in his hand and a disapproving

51

preacher at his side. The marshal stood near the door, his arm in a sling. His younger brother leant against the wall. He was now the active lawman and was attending a council meeting for the first time. The others were all seated: three lawyers, the judge, the banker, Doc Mason, and several of the more important store-owners.

'Well, folks, all the business of the day bein' over,' the mayor said in his official voice, 'I reckon as how we all sympathize with the marshal here, and wish him well. Larry's takin' over the job and I'm sure you all agree that he'll make a fine marshal.'

There was a reluctant nodding of heads and young Larry grinned at his wounded brother.

'You can surely go back to work when your arm's healed, Matt?' one of the storekeepers suggested hopefully.

'The doc reckons not, and I aim to retire, anyways. This marshallin' business is a young fella's game. I'll be well out of it.'

'Well, you and Larry sure dealt with them two Yankee fellas,' the mayor said cheerfully. 'Maybe we can all go back to normal now.'

He looked around, hoping that the council meeting was coming to an end. One of the storekeepers cleared his throat noisily.

'What's all this business about Tom Wallace sellin' off the hotel to Ralph Loman?' he asked. 'He's even talkin' about leavin' town. That don't sound right comin' from one of our earliest settlers. I asked his wife about it when she came into the store, but she didn't have nothin' to say. And that sure as hell ain't usual for Betty Wallace.'

The mayor looked around the room and leaned forward across the desk as though ready to impart a secret.

'Tom Wallace ain't goin' because he wants to,' he said in a low voice. 'It's Betty. She has a son and grandchildren up near the Gila, and these folks have quite a spread of cattle and horses in the area. She wants to be near him and his family. Tom ain't a fella to refuse his wife, so he's got rid of the hotel. Jim here is sellin' the house for him, and they'll be movin' out pretty soon.'

'I never knew Ma Wallace had been married before,' the preacher said in his starchiest voice.

'She was widowed in the war and left with a small boy,' the mayor explained. 'She ain't livin' in sin if that's what's sourin' your face. She met Tom and they got married when he moved here. He financed her son, and now they're gonna retire to the ranch. I reckon it's a pretty good way to end your days.'

Banker Moorcroft leaned forward.

'I can't talk about clients,' he said in his rich, pompous voice, 'but there is something about all this that has me mightily puzzled.'

The others all listened eagerly. They knew that Edwin Moorcroft, fat and pale-faced, loved talking about his clients. It demonstrated his own importance.

'And what would that be?' someone asked.

'Well, the first thing is, where did all the money come from? How in hell's name could Loman get that sort of cash? He doesn't have any dealings with me. And Tom Wallace hasn't paid any large sums into his account lately. I just can't figure it out.'

They all looked at Lawyer Roberts. His thin, hunched figure sat like a bird of prey.

'Ain't no secret,' he said in his dry, rasping voice. 'I just drew up a contract that changed title to the business. No mention was made of money. I figure as how Loman put down some sort of cash deposit and is paying the rest by instalments. Tom's content with that, I guess. Doesn't include no banking and no legal advice. Just a handshake between two fellas who trust each other. Not my idea of doing business, but Tom and Ralph Loman have worked together long enough to know what they're doing.'

The mayor stood up to indicate that the meeting was over. The others began to move off but Edwin Moorcroft remained seated. The mayor looked at him with an impatience that was obvious to all in the room.

'What's eatin' you, Edwin?' he asked.

'There's a fella in town who's staying at the Beauregard. I gather that his name is Donovan.'

'I've seen him around.' Davy Smith nodded. 'Big city fella by the cut of his clothes. So what about him?'

'We got into conversation over at the Southern Star the other day. He's supposed to be in the copper-mining business, so he says. My guess is that he knows as much about copper-mining as I do about church architecture. He certainly hasn't used the bank since he's been here.'

'And he hasn't been to the meeting-house,' the preacher said sourly.

Lawyer Roberts did not want to be left out. He shook his head mournfully.

'I've had no business dealings with him,' he said.

The old judge drained his whiskey

glass and gave a dry, cynical chuckle.

'Well, there ain't much wrong with a fella who keeps away from money-lenders, preachers, and lawyers. I must make his acquaintance.'

'He won't be good company. He doesn't drink the way you do,' the banker said spitefully. He looked round at the others. 'Could he be some sort of government man?' he asked.

'What the hell would a government fella be doin' skulkin' around here?' the mayor asked in slight alarm. 'We ain't the most popular town with the Washington crowd, but at least they leave us alone.'

'It's Jeff Davis's birthday next week and maybe they haven't forgotten the celebrations we held last year. All them firecrackers and parades. We hit all the journals for hundreds of miles around. The Washington lot don't like that sort of thing. We even got a mention in the Senate for sending greetings to Jeff Davis and his wife. He may be here to take notes of what we do this year. Just to make sure that nobody involved gets into the legislature.'

The mayor burst out laughing and was joined by most of the others. The banker did not find it in the least funny. He had secret ambitions of a political career.

'Well, I suppose our Mr Donovan will bear watching,' Davy Smith eventually conceded, 'but we sure as hell ain't gonna hide our loyalty to the South. Not in this town. The eighth of June is a day for celebration.

5

The new marshal had other things to do than watch Hank Donovan. He was noting every move made by Major Wallace. The retiring former hotel-owner no longer appeared in public. He stayed in his large house on the edge of town while his wife and servants did the chores. It was almost as though he did not want to see people who had once been his friends. A freight wagon arrived one morning and loaded up some of his furniture. It moved off a few hours later and headed north.

Marshal Larry Smith noted that the major's surrey was being made ready for a journey. He saw the horse being newly shod and stood watching from behind a wagon while Major Wallace and his wife climbed aboard. It was early morning and few people were about as they left town at a sedate pace.

They were following the route their household contents had taken a few days earlier.

The lawman's horse was ready and he also left town. Not to follow them yet. He knew where they were heading. He had other business to attend to.

He reached a wooden cabin after two hours of hard riding. It stood by a narrow creek and there were tall sycamores around it while three horses grazed in a small corral. They looked up with interest as someone new came on the scene. Larry Smith tethered his mount to the fence rail and slackened off the girth. He turned to find himself facing three men who stood in the doorway of the cabin with wide grins on their unshaven faces.

He shook hands with each of them in an almost formal fashion, and they led the way indoors. It was a rough cabin. A single lamp hung from the rotting roof and an old stove smoked as it brewed a pot of coffee. The occupiers were young men, two of them tall and thin, with dark faces and lank black hair that grew over their collars. The other was shorter and stouter with pale-blue eyes and scant hair of an unwashed brown. They stood round a rough table and a jar of corn mash was produced.

'Well, you sure is a sight for sore eyes,' the shorter one said as they drank. 'We was beginnin' to think you'd forgotten all about us.'

'A hell of a lot's been happenin' in town and there ain't been anythin' worth our attention,' Larry Smith said with a grin. 'Until now.'

One of the taller men peered hard at the marshal's waistcoat and leaned across to touch the badge he was wearing. Jeff Howard and his brother Brad had little respect for lawmen.

'Hey, fellas,' he crowed. 'We got ourselves a real live marshal here. Now ain't that a treat. No more deputizin' for our Larry.'

Everybody laughed although Larry Smith felt a little embarrassed. He explained his brother's injury and told a rather exaggerated tale of his own bravery under fire.

'So maybe that town of your'n will be wide open to us now,' the shorter man suggested slyly.

'Like hell it will. Every job I line up will be well away from Defiance. I gotta live there and control the place. You'll have nobody with a telegraph line and a Wells Fargo contact if I have to leave. So no trouble on my patch. Understood?'

They nodded reluctant agreement and sat down at the table to listen to the marshal's news.

'A fella's just left town,' Larry told them. 'He's one of our leadin' citizens and he's gone and sold his business and aims to settle on some cattle spread further north. I know the place he's headin' for and he's gotta have plenty of cash money on him. Whatever deposit he got for the hotel he sold wasn't paid into the local bank. He's carryin' it on him. His wife's also got a mass of jewellery that's worth takin' a shine to.'

'What's the split?' It was the stouter man who asked. Rob Downey was a few years older than the two brothers and was acknowledged to be the brains of the little gang.

'Even money. There'll be enough for all of us to live it up a little. It's just man and wife. They're drivin' a one-horse rig, travellin' slow. They have to keep to the trail so we can easily pass them, take the rig somewhere out among the mesquite.'

Rob nodded and rubbed his chin thoughtfully. 'Just the fella and his wife, you say,' he murmured. His eyes were hard as he stared at the marshal.

'Yeah, they'll be easy to pick off.'

'Well, you know, Larry, I'm thinkin' as how you're mighty generous to invite us along to this shindig when there's only a town dude and his wife to deal with. You could have done it all by yourself and saved havin' to split the take. Could there be somethin' you ain't tellin' us?'

Rob Downey grinned at the marshal

while the other two men looked suspicious. Larry Smith had the grace to shrug his shoulders as if defeated.

'Well, I guess it ain't quite so simple,' he admitted. 'This fella is no easy jackrabbit. He's an old soldier. In fact, he's a major who used to be in the Army of the Confederacy. A real shootin' man. And I hear tell his wife is handy with a gun as well. We're gonna earn that money.'

One of the young men clicked his fingers.

'Sounds like old Major Wallace,' he said. 'He's one of them soldier-boy heroes back in Defiance. I saw him once in a saloon there. But he sure as hell ain't no shootin' man. There's fingers missin' on one of his hands.'

'Not on his shootin' hand, Jeff,' Larry told him quietly. 'He uses the left one just as well. And a missin' eye don't seem to bother him none. I seen him at a turkey-shoot. Now, this is the plan I worked out. We ride ahead of them, stake out a good point, and bushwhack the rig. I had thought about trailin' them, but the ground's too dry and we'd raise one hell of a dust. We'll just ride until we catch sight of the rig. Then we'll circle the trail and be ahead of them when they make camp by Rossiter Creek. It's the obvious place for the first night. All agreed?'

There was a nodding of heads, but Rob Downey still had a question.

'Are we wearin' masks for this, or do you want them dead?' he asked shrewdly.

There was a silence that lasted for several seconds.

'I want them dead.' Larry Smith's voice was hard. 'And hidden off the trail. If you want to take the rig and the horse as your part of the deal, you can do so. But I don't want no travellers findin' the trail littered with bodies. Understand?'

'I'm not sure I like that,' Rob mused uneasily. 'I reckon we should get a better cut.'

He looked at the two brothers and

they took the hint with a murmur of agreement. Larry Smith hurriedly nodded.

'You can have the guns, baggage, and the rig,' he said. 'I'll just take my share of the money. Does that satisfy you?'

'I reckon. Let's get to horse.'

★   ★   ★

They rode for four hours before sighting the small surrey. It was bowling sedately along amid a trailing cloud of red dust. Major Wallace was driving while his wife sat in grim silence at his side. She was a stout woman who had once been a good-looker. Her hair was as grey as the major's but her eyes were a bright blue and keenly alert.

The two were hardly on speaking terms. Leaving the cosiness of Defiance to spend the rest of her life with her son and his family was not what Betty Wallace thought of as a comfortable old age. She knew that her husband was a former Yankee sergeant. She knew that his real name was Bedser. But she had been a widow with a growing boy. She needed safety, and that was what he represented.

Killing the freight hauler had been her idea. She was the tough one of the family. When the man had turned up at their house to say that he recognized her husband, she had reacted ruthlessly. While the two men talked and Tom had foolishly parted with fifty dollars, she had left the house in search of help.

Larry Smith did as she ordered. That was his job and he was well paid to protect the prominent people in town. The marshal was no good. He was too honest. But his brother was what was needed by those with something to protect. He did what was asked of him. It had gone wrong and the shot was not immediately fatal. The man had talked to that damned hotel manager. And they could not kill Ralph Loman. He was too crafty.

'We'll make camp along Rossiter Creek,' Tom said cheerfully. 'No point in tirin' the horses, and the water's good there. Those big mesquites will keep the wind off us too.'

Ma Wallace grunted. She was holding on to her veiled hat and inwardly cursing her fate. Her husband glanced at her.

'It's no use goin' on like this, Betty,' he said meekly. 'It's just somethin' we couldn't foresee, and I couldn't stay in that town with folk talkin' and wonderin' about why we sold the hotel. If I believed in a god, I'd think it was his way of gettin' even with me.'

'We could have stayed,' she snapped angrily. 'That Loman fella left letters with the bank and with his lawyer. Young Larry Smith could have got them letters back and killed Loman. We just needed to stick it out for a while and be ready to take a few risks. We've lost everythin' now, thanks to you.'

He shook his head. 'I don't think even Larry would have the nerve to go raidin' a bank,' he said. 'And suppose the letters were locked up in the safe.

He's a lawman, for Pete's sake, not a bank-robber. He couldn't kill Loman until he was sure of gettin' the letters, and if it went wrong, we'd have had Loman screamin' his head off to beat the band. We'd have been lynched as soon as he raised the alarm.'

'You'd have been lynched,' his wife pointed out unkindly. 'I'd have just been a poor, deceived Southern widow who managed to take up with some dishonest Yankee.'

They looked at each other for a moment and then the tension vanished. Major Wallace burst out laughing and his wife joined in. They drove on in companionable silence.

Rossiter Creek had been named after an old miner who had found its sweet water some forty years earlier. It came out fresh and clear after being filtered through layers of sand. There was tall mesquite all round that swayed in the stiff breeze. It made a swishing noise as it shed dust in erratic showers.

They unharnessed the horse and set

it to graze with a hobble that was hardly necessary. While Ma Wallace unpacked their bedding, Tom lit a fire, put some water in the coffee-pot and a large pan, and set them to heat.

Their meal was a simple one. There was no maidservant now. She had been left behind. Betty Wallace had to clean the tin dishes herself. It was an easy enough job as she rubbed the plates with sand and packed them away again. Dusk had long since fallen and the fire lit up their world. Moths were gathering above the flames and nocturnal creatures began to scuttle around in the quickly gathering darkness.

It was Tom who heard the slight sound and his head arched as he listened hard. He held a warning finger to his lips and reached for the gun under his coat. Betty stood up with a casual air, stretched herself, and wandered over to the surrey. She reached in and her questing fingers found the shotgun she was seeking. She swung around, the double-barrelled weapon cocked and ready to use.

Two shadows appeared out of the darkness at the other side of the fire. Her husband turned to confront them. His gun was unholstered and the clicking of the hammer was loud in the sudden hush that had fallen. Then he relaxed and waved the pistol to indicate to his wife that all was well.

'It's all right, Ma,' he said with relief in his voice. 'it's Larry Smith.'

The marshal stepped into the fire-light. Rob Downey was at his side and both men grinned as they approached.

'And what brings you out to this spot, Larry?' Tom Wallace asked in his best Confederate accent.

'I heard tell that you'd left town,' the new marshal said as he looked keenly around. 'It seems a pity to go without sayin' goodbye to the folks that have helped you, Major. I still don't know why you wanted that fella dead. I reckon it ain't my business. But you sellin' the hotel and movin' out so soon afterwards, well, that sure had me puzzlin' over things, you know.'

'Oh, I just decided to retire, Larry,' Tom said with a smile that did not reach his eyes. 'Running a business and living in a town was getting too much for an old fella like me.'

Tom Wallace's voice was still cheery but there was an edge of worry to it. Something in the marshal's manner warned him that this was not a friendly call.

'I hear tell that no money was paid into the bank when you sold out to Ralph Loman,' Larry Smith said tautly.

'Well, Ralph and me is old friends, and he's going to pay me by instalments.'

'So I heard tell. But I calculate that he'd lay down some sort of deposit. That's the usual way things get done. At least, that's what the bankin' fella seems to think. Carryin' a parcel of ready cash can be a pretty dangerous way of goin' about things. You could be bushwhacked on the trail.'

'Oh, I ain't carryin' much. Just

travelling money.'

Tom Wallace was now conscious of two more figures somewhere to his right. He could see the vague movements but was keeping his eye on the lawman in front of him. He knew what their game was now. He and his wife were going to be robbed. And they would be mighty lucky not to be murdered.

'Betty and me just want to get away peaceful-like,' he said in a meek voice and without worrying about his accent any more. 'We're old folk, Larry, and ain't got much left in life.'

'I reckon that's the case.'

There was a snigger from the shadows on Tom Wallace's right. They were closer now and he could see two youngish men armed with Winchesters. It was Betty who made the decision. She levelled the shotgun and let one barrel fly. The blast deafened the ears and a cloud of hovering insects rose from around the fire.

Rob Downey staggered backwards.

His face was blown away by the shot and he fell to the ground. Larry Smith drew his gun and was almost beaten to the draw by Tom Wallace. The bogus major had put the Colt back under his coat and was now not quite fast enough. They both managed to fire at much the same time, but Tom Wallace missed. He took a shot in the neck and reeled back a few yards before falling. The pistol dropped from his hand.

His wife swung her gun at the other two men. They had brought up the Winchesters and both fired from the hip. One shot caught her in the side and the shotgun blasted the air to slaughter a few moths. She went down on her knees and another shot finished her.

A short silence followed. Larry Smith grinned at his two remaining colleagues.

'I reckon we've earned ourselves a few dollars,' he said happily. 'Too bad about Rob.'

'A three-way split is better than four,' one of the others laughed. He bent over

Betty Wallace and began taking the rings from her fingers.

They searched the dead man's body and ransacked the baggage on the surrey. All that turned up was a couple of hundred dollars and a few trinkets like watches and silver candlesticks. The three men looked at each other in disgust.

'So where's all this cash money he was carryin' outa town?' Jeff Howard asked the marshal suspiciously.

Larry shook his head. 'I can't understand it,' he muttered. 'If he sold that hotel, he must have been paid somethin' on account.' He looked round uncertainly.

'We'll just have to be content with what we've got. Let's hide these bodies off the trail and get the hell outa here. You fellas can take whatever you want. But sell it well away from Defiance. Then lie low and I'll come visit you as soon as I hear of somethin' worth our while.'

6

Hank Donovan left the Beauregard Hotel quite early and walked down the main street at a leisurely pace. His actions were deceptive. This well-fed and well-dressed visitor was looking around shrewdly. He noted every person on the street and every move that occurred. The jailhouse was locked up and there was no sign of the new marshal.

He came to the north end of town, turned left into one of the side lanes and found himself behind the house of Major Wallace. The place looked deserted and Hank Donovan frowned. He glanced at the corral where the Wallace horse was usually kept. It was missing, and so was the surrey that it so often drew. The large man bit his lip angrily as he quickened his pace to go round to the front of the building.

The blinds were drawn and he hesitated before deciding to walk up the gravelled path and knock at the white front door. He waited impatiently but there was no answer. He gave vent to a muttered curse and turned on his heel to hurry back to the hotel.

Ralph Loman was in his office when the door burst open and he was confronted by one of his guests.

'Mr Donovan,' he protested. 'This is not the way — '

'Where's Tom Wallace?' The words were snapped at him in an angry tone that boded trouble.

'Well, I don't know,' Loman muttered uncomfortably. 'He and his wife live at the far end of town. They're not my concern any more. Really, Mr Donovan . . .'

The visitor was standing over him and looking menacing. The hotel-owner could see the butt of a gun sticking out from under the frock-coat. He gulped noisily.

'How can I help?' he asked meekly.

'Where have they gone? And when?'

'Well, I really think that's a matter for them, Mr Donovan.'

The big man pulled up a bentwood chair and sat down. He leaned his heavy body across the desk and glared at the owner.

'Now, let's you and me get a few things straight, Mr Loman,' he said tersely. 'You sent a letter to Washington a few months back. You wanted information on a Sergeant Bedser. Are we understandin' each other a little better now?'

The little man gulped again. 'Are you a government man, Mr Donovan?' he asked in a quavering voice.

'I'm a federal marshal, Mr Loman, and it just happens that the government of these United States is also interested in Sergeant Bedser, now called Major Wallace. So I suggest you start talkin' if you want to stay out of the jailhouse.'

'I didn't do nothin' wrong,' the elderly man pleaded in the whining voice he had used in his days of management.

'But when a dyin' man mentions a name and then I see the discharge papers, well, what was I to think?'

'Go on.'

Ralph Loman told about his friend who worked as a clerk in a government office. He had asked him to check on this mysterious sergeant and received the news about his theft and desertion.

'It was so easy,' he sighed. 'He wrote me about the war wound and I knew right away that it was Major Wallace. There couldn't be any doubt.'

'So you made him sell out to you and forced him to leave town?'

'I didn't force him to leave. I didn't even know he was aimin' to up stakes like that. I just wanted to be somebody at last. And this fella was as phoney as a whiskey-drummer sellin' high wines. He could afford to let me have this place, and I weren't aimin' to tell the town what he'd done.'

Donovan leaned back in his chair and smiled cruelly at the sweating hotel-owner.

'Mr Loman,' he said softly, 'you're either a very brave man or a very stupid one. I reckon as how you ain't gonna live much longer. So enjoy it while you can.'

Ralph Loman pulled himself upright and managed a thin smile of pride.

'I ain't pretendin' to be brave,' he said, 'but I'm not stupid. I've left letters with two important people in town. If the major had killed me the way he had that other fella killed, those letters would have been opened. And they told everythin' about what was happenin' in Defiance.'

Donovan's grin grew wider. 'Mr Loman,' he said, 'your Sergeant Bedser couldn't have stolen a pair of old boots unless he had someone more intelligent to help him. Bedser was just a wounded hero who was given an easy job in an office. Somebody else helped to steal that payroll. Somebody who knew how to work things so that they had time to get the job done and be away before anything was discovered. Not the sergeant's style, at all. It was a neat operation but he nearly spoiled it by killin' two fellas. Then he just carried the loot and led everybody on a false trail. That's why you're in trouble. The real fella is still in town, and he must know all about you. Bedser will have told him.'

Ralph Loman sat rigidly in his chair. The colour drained out of his face as he thought about it. He opened his mouth to speak but no words came out. A bead of sweat gathered on his forehead.

'Who is it?' he asked after a while.

'That's what I have to find out, Mr Loman. And with Sergeant Bedser leavin' town, you're my only lead. I'll just have to hang around until somebody kills you.'

'I've got them letters with my lawyer and in the bank,' the little man said eagerly. 'They'll keep me safe.'

Donovan shook his head. 'They tell us about Bedser,' he pointed out. 'But not about his partner. And if your banker or your lawyer happens to be the partner, you ain't got a lotta help there. You see, Ralph, if that partner thinks you've any idea that he's involved, he's gonna come gunnin' for you as sure as John Wilkes Booth went gunnin' for Lincoln.'

The hotel owner swallowed noisily. 'What can I do?' he asked anxiously.

'Well, you can start by tellin' me where Bedser's gone. Every detail.'

The little man was eager to help. He told the federal marshal about Ma Wallace's son and the ranch up on the Gila. Donovan listened carefully.

'I don't know when they left though,' Ralph Loman said. 'He sent most of the furniture off the other day and got rid of the hired help. But he's been keepin' himself to himself lately. I thought he was just ashamed to look folks in the eye. I would never have said anythin' but I figured as how he just didn't trust me.'

'So I should find him at his stepson's place?'

'I guess so, but will he tell you who his partner is?'

'I'll just have to see what I can do. Now tell me, Ralph, who did he speak to after you got this hotel off'n him?'

'Well, he went to his lawyer to fix up the deeds. And I know he went to the bank for some reason. He didn't go into the saloon no more, but he paid a visit on the mayor and he went to the meetin' house every Sunday like always. Didn't seem to want to speak to folks, though. Then he had to see Doc Mason about his regular aches and pains. And he was at the smithy once or twice.' He thought for a moment. 'And I think I saw him talkin' to the judge. Why do you ask?'

'One of the folks he spoke to would probably have been his partner. And your name might just have got a mention. It's worth thinkin' about, Ralph. I reckon that new marshal could be gettin' orders any day now. Just as a matter of interest, how much did you pay him for this place?'

'Not a lot.'

'How much?' The voice was menacing.

'Five dollars.'

'Could be the most expensive purchase you ever made.' Hank Donovan got up to leave. His chair scraped noisily on the floor.

'You're not leavin' town?' the hotel man asked fearfully.

Hank Donovan appeared to think about it for a moment.

'No, not yet,' he said slowly. 'I'll do a deal with you, Ralph. You keep quiet about who I am, and I'll stick around and try and keep you alive for a while. If anyone asks about me, put the word around that I'm checkin' the area for seams of copper. There are some instruments in my baggage that will bear that out, and I've already let hints drop to folks who got curious in the saloon. Understood?'

'Yes, yes, Marshal. I understand.'

'I've got my eye on one or two folks in town, but I don't want anybody runnin' scared just yet.'

'Marshal, I don't want to try tellin' you your job, but I would suggest that the man you want will be one of our earlier settlers. And a wealthy one at that.'

'That had crossed my mind. Most of the storekeepers and near every councilman comes into that group. And most of them are about the right age. You'll surely have to watch your back.'

He crossed to the door when another thought struck him.

'This new marshal was takin' orders from Bedser,' he mused. 'What about the older lawman? Do you reckon he was doin' the same?'

Ralph Loman shook his head.

'I wouldn't imagine so. Matt Smith is a straight sorta fella. He don't like too much work, but I never heard tell that he did anythin' that weren't honest. I'd like to think he'd come back when his wound's healed, but the word is out that he's retiring.'

'So I heard tell. How does he get on with his brother?'

Loman shrugged. 'They ain't close,' he said. 'I think maybe Matt knows that Larry is a no-good bum. They just about stay civil to each other.'

★   ★   ★

Hank Donovan sat on the porch of the Beauregard Hotel. The afternoon sun was warm and he appeared to be reading a newspaper. He was in reality watching the street. Somewhere among all these people was the man he really wanted. The man who had organized a complicated robbery, the killing of two clerks in the process, and the use of a wounded sergeant to act as a front for him.

He saw Larry Smith ride into town and open up the jailhouse. The man looked as if he'd travelled some distance. Hank Donovan watched as the marshal emerged a few minutes later and went across to the saloon. He did think about going there himself but changed his mind when he saw that the lawman was sitting down near a window and was being served with a meal.

The federal marshal had little doubt that the peace officer of Defiance would lead him to the man he was after. It was just a matter of time and patience. Nobody in town could be trusted if they were of an age to have been in the late war. He sighed and went back to reading the paper.

* * *

The town was silent and dark at two o'clock in the morning. Bats flew in deadly sweeps at insects in their paths while rats scuttled along the lanes. A horse or mule made an occasional noise and somewhere down by the creek a lone prairie-wolf was calling to the moon.

Two shadows moved behind the office of Lawyer Roberts. They were tall, slim men who quietly opened the back door with a bunch of keys that rattled softly against the woodwork. They entered the place and felt their way along the walls of the corridor until they came to the lawyer's room. One of the men took a small lantern from under his shirt and placed it on the desk. It was a shaded box of tin with a candle-stub which he lit with a vesta. It threw a narrow light on the safe and his companion went across and had the thing open with an ease that set both men grinning widely.

Jeff and Brad Howard crouched over the bundles of papers and eventually got what they wanted. They found some money as well and took that for good measure. Then they left the building as quietly as they had entered it.

The bank was their next call. Another bunch of keys opened the heavy rear door and they were soon in front of the large safe in the manager's office. The tiny lantern was lit again while Jeff picked out the key he wanted. It took only a matter of seconds to pull open the door and disclose the rows of banknotes that lay invitingly on two shelves. Brad pulled a small cotton bag from his shirt and began to pile in the money. His brother was looking for something else and let out a little grunt of satisfaction when he found it. They closed the safe quietly, left the keys in the lock, and headed back for the rear door.

The moon threw their shadows harshly across the stoop as they emerged. It also threw another shadow. A man was standing a few yards away. It was Larry Smith, and he held a shotgun that was pointing at the two brothers.

'You got 'em?' he asked tersely.

'Sure did, boss.' Jeff held out the envelopes while his brother gleefully waved the bag of money.

'That's all I need to know,' the lawman said in a happier voice. He pulled the triggers, one after the other, and the blasts took both men, one in the chest and one in the head. They stumbled backwards, their arms flailing and their legs giving way as they fell against the wall of the bank.

Larry Smith looked quickly around and then made sure that both were dead. He tucked the envelopes into his shirt, pulled the guns from the holsters of his victims, and laid them on the wooden porch next to the bodies. Then he stood back and waited.

He did not have long to wait. The crowd gathered as noisily and quickly as if a circus had come to town. The mayor pushed his way through, followed by the mortician and a panting Doctor Mason. The medical man looked at the fallen bandits, shook his head sadly, and did not bother to open his black bag.

'They're all yours, Abner,' he said to the mortician.

The mayor took Larry Smith by the arm and led him to a corner beyond the gathering crowd. The judge and a couple of councilmen tagged along. They had dressed hastily and the judge was still searching his pocket for the gold-rimmed glasses he usually wore.

'So what happened, Larry?' the mayor asked his cousin.

'I was just doin' one more tour of the town before turnin' in for the night when I thought I saw a light in the bank. I couldn't be certain and there were no horses around. I just stood on the corner of the lane and waited.'

The marshal chuckled modestly. 'I was beginnin' to feel one almighty fool when the back door opens and out they come. I challenged them and they drew on me pretty fast. I didn't do no arguin' about it. Just let fly, Cousin Davy.'

'And the right thing to do,' the mayor agreed while all the others nodded their approval. 'You sure as hell saved the bank's cash. And that's an interestin' thing. Where the hell is our money-lendin' friend?'

There was no sign of the banker. The mayor led the way to his house at the other end of the main street. Quite a few people followed the little procession, and Ralph Loman was among them. He found himself walking next to one of the guests at his hotel. Hank Donovan was extremely interested in all that was happening.

The banker and his wife were soon found. They sat in chairs, tightly bound and gagged. They had been wakened by the Howard brothers and the bank keys taken from them. The mayor had no sooner emerged into the night again when somebody brought news that the back door of the lawyer's house was wide open. He and his wife were also found tied up and gagged. His office keys had been taken and his scrawny wife was complaining bitterly about a gold-and-diamond cameo the thieves had also removed.

The news soon reached the crowd of people who had followed the mayoral procession. Hank Donovan looked at Ralph Loman and smiled slightly.

'I reckon those two envelopes have just gone missing,' he said softly. 'I hope you're carryin' a gun, Ralph.'

The hotel owner gulped and decided

to leave the street and hurry back to the hotel.

Had he stayed around a little longer and looked through the windows of the jailhouse, he would have been able to see the marshal of Defiance reading what was in the two envelopes and then putting them in the stove. They helped to heat his celebration coffee.

7

Marshal Smith was the hero of Defiance. The bank had been saved and the raiders were dead. The council voted their lawman a bonus of twenty dollars and everyone was eager to buy him a drink.

Hank Donovan watched it all with a certain puzzlement. He knew why everything had happened but could not pin down the man he really wanted. He guessed that the two bandits had been working with Larry Smith. That was the only thing that explained the raid on the office of Lawyer Roberts as well as on the bank. He felt certain that Ralph Loman would be an eventual target once the letters were safely destroyed. Bedser must have given all the details to his mysterious partner before he left town, and now the man was making sure that nothing could be traced back.

Hank Donovan desperately wanted to go north to the place where Bedser and his wife had decided to settle. He could bring enough pressure on the ex-sergeant to get the name of his partner. But he felt that he had to wait in Defiance to see if any move was made against the new owner of the Beauregard Hotel. He watched everything that happened in the town and wished that his bosses had seen fit to send him more help.

A couple of weeks went past and Larry Smith eventually had to buy his own drinks. All the excitement settled down and the latest gossip was of the school-ma'am and the blacksmith's son. It was much more entertaining than a bank robbery.

Nobody paid any attention to the young man who rode into town late one afternoon and stopped at the Southern Star saloon for a drink and a meal. He enquired about a rooming-house and ended up at Ma Blane's comfortable place. It was in one of the side lanes down by the livery and feed-stores.

The young visitor was tall and rangy, with an open face and fair, short hair. He carried a gun at his side and there was a Winchester in his saddle holster. His clothes were clean and he was freshly shaven. There was an honesty in his expression but also a certain toughness that bespoke a man who was not afraid of life.

The day after his arrival in town was a Sunday. Ralph Loman went scurrying down the main street towards the meeting-house as usual. He carried a prayer-book and joined the singing and praying in much the same way as he had done for years. He was a model citizen, and now featured among the more important people in town.

He hurried back to the Beauregard Hotel when it was all over. His stooped, unctuous posture could not really change after so many years, and he now gave nervous glances to right and left as he moved. The hotel-owner was still not sure about his safety. He saw Hank

Donovan sitting on the stoop with a cigar in his mouth. That cheered him a little and he nodded to the federal marshal as he entered the building.

Somebody else was watching. The young stranger strolled quietly round to the back of the hotel and tried the rear door. It was not locked and he entered quietly. There was a kitchen to his left with somebody moving about there and a smell of cooking. To his right was an open door that showed a storeroom with blankets and cleaning-materials on wide shelves. He went on down the carpeted corridor and entered the foyer of the hotel. The stairs confronted him, with the reception desk just to the left. There was nobody on duty and no guests occupied any of the tables or leather armchairs.

There was a slightly more imposing door behind the desk. It bore the name of the new owner in fresh gold lettering. The young man turned the brass knob and entered the room.

Ralph Loman was at his desk. He

had just poured himself a cup of coffee and held it in both hands. The sudden appearance of a stranger shook his already taut nerves. The hot liquid spilled on to the desk and the little man retreated a step or two until his back was against the wall.

'Who — who are you?' he asked fearfully. 'I don't know you.'

The young man closed the door gently behind him and advanced to the desk.

'I'm Bill Danvers,' he said quietly, 'and I want to know where my ma and pa have gotten to. You'd know my ma as Mrs Wallace. The major's wife. So where is she, fella?'

'Well, I — I don't know,' Ralph Loman stuttered. 'Her and the major left here a coupla weeks back. They was supposed to be headin' for your place. They must be there by now. It's only a three or four days' journey.'

'They ain't turned up. You got any ideas about that?'

The voice was quietly menacing but

Ralph Loman was a little less frightened now that he knew who the young man was. He sat down at the desk and tried to regain his composure.

'They sent off their furniture a few days before they left themselves,' he said. 'Then they went off early one mornin' in the surrey. Just never said nothin' to nobody. That's all I know about them, fella. Maybe they decided to go some other place. Your ma was real upset at movin' out, but — '

'I know all about my stepfather, Mr Loman,' Bill Danvers said wryly. 'He was some sort of thief who set up as a Confederate major until you got on to him. You did a good job of it, fella. Y'see he wrote me a letter, tellin' all about you takin' this place off him for five dollars and scarin' him outa town. You sure were one smart operator. He couldn't get outa this place fast enough. Now, I'll tell you, fella. I don't give a damn about him. But I do about my ma. And if you've done any harm to her, I'm gonna kill you.'

Ralph Loman was sweating. He shook his head violently and tried to give an ingratiating smile.

'I just bought this place off him,' he said hurriedly. 'I had no reason to do either of them any harm. But I was glad when he decided to leave town. It seemed the best thing. They've got to be somewhere around. Two people and a horse-drawn rig can't vanish between here and your place.'

'Well, they have. Their furniture arrived. And then we waited. I back-trailed them but there's no sign of a rig between here and my spread. They've just plumb vanished. Do any of the folks round here know that he's a Bluebelly deserter who stole a payroll?'

'No. He played the part of a major to the last. And I sure as hell don't aim to spread the word.'

'He told me in the letter about some fella tryin' to get money outa him. Then the fella got drunk and your lawman had to shoot him. Is that what happened?'

'More or less.'

Ralph Loman explained how the dying freight-hauler had spoken of a Sergeant Bedser and how information had been obtained from Washington. Bill Danvers listened patiently. Then he suddenly reached across the desk and grabbed the hotel man by the collar.

He hauled him to his feet and pulled him across so that their faces were within inches of each other.

'Have you told me the whole story, fella?' the young man asked in a hard voice.

Ralph Loman nodded violently. 'Every word!' he squealed. 'And I'll tell you somethin' else that folks round here don't know. There's a federal marshal in town and he reckons as how your stepfather had a partner. He aims to get them both.'

Bill Danvers released his hold on the little man.

'Is that a fact now?' he murmured. 'Then maybe this federal fella has already got him and he's in some jailhouse.'

'No, no.' Ralph Loman shook his head violently. 'The lawman ain't moved from town. He's sittin' out there on the stoop at this minute. He reckons as how the partner is more important than your step-pa. Reckons he's the real brains behind the robbery.'

'Well, that could be the truth. I never reckoned Tom for much in the way of brains. Maybe I oughta have a talk with this lawman.'

'That might be a good idea.'

The voice took Bill Danvers by surprise and his hand reached down for the gun at his hip. As he turned, he realized that Hank Donovan had already drawn his own Colt and had him covered. The big man had moved so quietly over the carpeted floor that Bill had not heard him enter the room.

The federal marshal used his left hand to display a badge that was housed in a leather wallet. He motioned young Bill Danvers to move round to the other side of the desk next to Ralph Loman.

'I do a little listenin' at keyholes now

and then,' the federal man said with a grin, 'and I hear tell that you're Sergeant Bedser's stepson. Can you prove that?'

Bill nodded and put a hand into the pocket of his shirt.

'This is Tom's letter,' he said, 'tellin' me that he and my ma was comin' to live with us.'

He held it out but the lawman again made a gesture with the gun.

'Mr Loman can look at it,' he said.

The hotel owner obliged with trembling fingers. He nodded his agreement that it was the genuine article and the lawman put away his gun.

'Then it would appear we're all on the same side,' he said. 'Ralph here wants to stay alive. You want to find your folks. And I want to catch the fella who masterminded the whole caboodle. We all need to help each other.'

The lawman looked carefully at the two men. Then he nodded to young Bill Danvers.

'I reckon as how you and me should

go some place quiet and have a talk,' he said. 'We can leave Ralph here in peace to enjoy bein' a big man in a small town.'

He held open the door and ushered the young man out to the foyer. They were both silent as he led the way to his own room and closed the door firmly behind them.

'You back-trailed your folk,' he said. 'How well did you do it, lad?'

Bill shrugged. 'I ain't no tracker, Marshal,' he admitted. 'I just came by way of the trail they'd have to take to get to my place. No signs of them.'

Donovan nodded thoughtfully. 'It could be that they went elsewhere,' he mused, 'but I somehow doubt it. Let's figure it out reasonably. The fella I'm after is here in town. He controls the new marshal. If the lawman was watchin' your folks, he'd follow them carefully and do the bush-whackin' as close to home as he could. He wouldn't want to be too long away from Defiance. And the place to lay a trap is where they'd stop for the first night. Are you with me?'

The young man nodded. 'That place where the water filters up through the sand. I think they call it Rossiter Creek.'

'That's where I'd choose. Far enough from Defiance to be safe, but not too far.'

'I stopped there myself on the way into town. There were signs of old fires but no wheel marks or anythin' that told a story.'

'It's too long ago, lad. I suggest you and me ride out there. Can you use that gun?'

'If I have to.'

'Good. I could do with some back-up. I ain't got no friends in this town and Washington don't seem anxious to help. We'll wait till dark and set out quietly. I don't want that marshal fella trailin' us.'

★   ★   ★

It was a moonlit night but the two men had to make camp eventually or they

105

would have lost the trail. There was no water and no cover from the sharp, dry wind. All they could do was to wear their trail coats and wrap horse-blankets round themselves as they dozed fitfully until the sun rose and the sounds and creatures of the night faded away.

They set out again, the sun getting hotter and the wind dropping. It was noon when they reached Rossiter Creek. Bill lit a fire while the marshal searched among the ashes left by other visitors. He poked through the dust-covered cinders and looked among the roots of the surrounding plants for any clues.

There was nothing of interest and he stood at the side of the creek, looking around absently as his young compan-ion fried bacon and made coffee. Then something caught his eye and he bent down to tug at a piece of rope that was partly buried in the reddish sand.

'What is it?' Bill had seen the older man's sudden alertness and watched with interest as he displayed a short piece of hemp that was looped at one end.

'It's part of a hobble,' the lawman said softly, 'and somebody didn't bother to keep it. It don't look damaged. Just one end untied. Why throw it away?'

'Tom always had a hobble in that surrey he bought for Ma,' Bill said. 'I recall as how he told us that it was old army trainin' from way back. Like some fool, I thought he meant the Confederate army.'

'When did you find out that he was a Northerner?'

'As I grew up a bit. That phoney accent would slip at home, and he and Ma laughed about him bein' an uppity major with all the folks kissin' his butt in admiration. That's why I left home when I got married. Wanted to be away from it all.'

'I'm told he financed you.'

'He sure did. And I was glad of his help. But I paid him back, Mr

Donovan. Every bent cent. I ain't denyin' he was good to me and Ma, but I always figured him for somethin' I'd rather not grow up to be.'

The federal marshal had moved to the other side of the creek. He was scanning the ground closely and his coat brushed against the mesquite to send showers of dust into the air. He suddenly let out a little gasp and went down on one knee. His right hand moved across the ground carefully, disturbing the topsoil and grit that littered it.

'What have you found?' his young companion asked anxiously.

'There have been animals around this spot. They've left plenty of tracks. I'm lookin' for what brought them here. It had to be somethin' eatable.'

His hand suddenly stopped. It was half-buried in the sand. He turned to look up at Bill Danvers.

'Maybe you'd like to go tend the horses,' he suggested gently, 'and leave this to me.'

'You've found them?'

'I reckon so. There's cloth here, son. There won't be much else after this time. Just bones. Between the animals and the insects, not a lot survives in this sort of place. Can you take this?'

Bill nodded. 'I have to,' he said. 'I ain't got a choice.'

The two men worked for a while, scooping out sand and soil until a pile of torn rags and some bones lay in front of them. It was plain that there were three skeletons, and some of the clothing was that of a woman. The two men sat silently when they had done all they could. There were tears in the young man's eyes and even the experienced lawman was looking solemn.

'Looks like your folks did a bit of shootin' themselves,' Hank Donovan eventually said quietly. 'This here skull is full of buckshot, and what's left of the clothes suggests we got ourselves one fella dressed like a cowpoke. Your step-pa was wearin' what looks like a cutaway coat with a tailor's tab inside it. And there's a starched collar on his skeleton. Real town fella, he was.'

'So what do we do now, Marshal?' Bill asked miserably.

'Well, I reckon as how we gets ready to start shootin' at whoever is watchin' us from behind them bushes.'

8

The marshal swung round. The Colt seemed to fly into his hand as he faced the large patch of scrub to his right. There were two tall clumps of cactus-bushes that stood like sentinels behind the lower masses of dust-covered plants. He fired a single shot and was greeted by a yell of pain or fright.

Bill Danvers had also drawn. He was slower but was able to get off two shots into the mass of greenery. He could not see any target but knew that shooting was necessary.

A figure staggered out of the bushes, sending up a cloud of dust. It was a thickset man with a greying beard and wild eyes. He swayed awkwardly as he drew a gun as if in some sort of trance. Hank Donovan fired again and the man dropped. The second shot had hardly been needed. The dead man's movements had been pure reaction.

There was a moment of silence and then the sound of bushes being shoved apart as somebody fled from the scene. Bill Danvers pushed his way through the scrub and saw two horses hitched to a small tree about thirty yards away at the bottom of a slope. A man was running towards them. He was taller than his dead companion, poorly dressed and limping slightly as he ran. Bill fired but the range was too great. Hank Donovan aimed more carefully and tried a shot. He too missed and cursed vividly.

Bill ran towards his own horse and unholstered the Winchester. He sped back to where Hank Donovan was reloading. The federal marshal shouted something to him as he raised the weapon and aimed carefully at the running man. He could not hear what Hank Donovan said in the excitement, but pulled the trigger as soon as he was sure of his target.

The running man staggered for a moment, recovered, and was almost reaching for the bridle of his mount when he slowly sank to the earth. Bill let out a whoop and turned to accept the praise of the federal marshal.

'I told you to shoot the damned horses,' Hank Donovan snapped. 'I wanted that fella alive so that he could answer a few questions.'

Bill was humiliated. 'Sorry, Marshal,' he said, 'but I just didn't hear you, I guess. I ain't used to havin' folks shootin' at me like you.'

The lawman relented and his brow cleared.

'No, I suppose not. But with a kick in the right place, he might have told us a few interestin' things. I reckon as how that marshal back in Defiance sent these two fellas after us.'

'To kill us?'

'Maybe not, but he'd sure as hell like to know what a coupla strangers are doin' on his patch.'

Hank Donovan examined the body of

the man he had himself shot. He was quite dead. He walked round the clumps of bushes and cacti to make his way down the slope where the other man lay. This one was on his face within a few feet of the horses. He was breathing in shallow gasps but it was obvious that he had not very long to live. There was no way he was going to talk to the lawman.

'Well, now we got ourselves an interestin' situation,' Hank said thoughtfully. 'What story do we tell when we get back to town?'

'We could take on that lawman,' Bill said angrily. 'He has to be back of all this. I reckon we both know that he killed my ma.'

'He did, son. I don't doubt it. But he's only the gun. It's the fella behind him we need. And goin' at things all wild and General Custer-like ain't gonna do us a lotta good. We're on our own in this. You want to get even for your kin and I want a fella what took off with a government payroll and killed two soldiers. We gotta play it real careful.'

He looked at the young man and then down at the body of the stranger. His lips were pursed in thought as he began to untether the two horses. He smacked each one on the rump and they took off at a happy pace as though they were glad to be free of human company.

'Now I think we ought to get back to town and take your kin with us for a proper burial. But you gotta follow my lead, and do as I say. If we make a wrong move, we might just meet a few more friends of the marshal. And I might not hear them comin' next time.'

*   *   *

Defiance was quiet and peaceful in the cool of the early evening and a few lights were going on. Marshal Larry Smith sat in his office drinking coffee. His new deputy stood at the bar of the Southern Star saloon.

Nobody paid much attention to Bill Danvers and Hank Donovan as they rode into town. They were now familiar figures and a few people nodded their greeting to the federal marshal. One elderly lady eyed the blankets that were parcelled up and hung from Bill's crupper like sacks. They looked odd but she passed by without comment.

The two men drew rein outside the jailhouse. They got wearily from their saddles and crossed the stoop to the warmth of the office. Larry Smith looked up in surprise as they entered. His face froze for a moment, he seemed stunned, and then rose uncertainly from his chair.

'What can I do for you gents?' he asked in a tense voice.

Hank Donovan was more at ease. He grinned at the lawman and gestured towards the doorway.

'We got a coupla bodies out there, Marshal,' he said cheerfully. 'Just thought you might like to know.'

Larry Smith opened his mouth to say

something. Then he bit back whatever it was. He headed for the door and his two visitors stood aside to let him pass. He blundered out on to the stoop and stared at the two weary horses.

'Where the hell are they?' he asked in puzzlement.

'In the blankets.'

The marshal turned angrily to face his visitors.

'Are you two fellas tryin' to be funny or something?' he asked harshly.

'They're wrapped up in them blankets, Marshal,' Hank Donovan said quietly. 'It's a man and a woman, and they've been dead for some time. We found them out at Rossiter Creek. They was buried there and the animals must have scattered the bones a bit when they was feeding. Thought we'd better bring them into town for a decent burial.'

'Yeah, yeah.' Larry Smith was trying to get his thoughts together. He had been expecting the bodies to be those of his hired help. When he saw

Donovan leaving town with young Bill Danvers, he had sent a couple of his friends to follow them. They had been given a strong hint that there was extra pay in it if the two strangers did not return to Defiance. Larry did not intend to take any chances in the big game that he was playing. But now here they were with what was left of the Wallaces. He could think of no other bodies coming from Rossiter Creek. He stood uncertainly for a moment and then pulled himself together.

'Yeah, well thanks for bringin' them in,' he murmured. 'If you'll just take them along to the mortician's parlour, I reckon the town can give them a decent burial.'

Hank Donovan raised a cynical eyebrow. 'They do need to be identified,' he suggested. 'Might be folks from this town or folks who was comin' here. Maybe the doctor had better look at them. And you could find out somethin' from the bits of clothing, perhaps.'

The marshal looked at the two men.

'Yeah, well, I guess we gotta try,' he said dubiously, 'but after all that time in the ground, there won't be much to check on, will there?'

The idea seemed to cheer him up but the smiling face of Hank Donovan upset his hopes of an easy way out.

'There's a label inside the fella's coat,' the federal man said quietly. 'They don't mean nothin' to me, but local folks might get some information from it. You want I should take them along to Doc Mason and let him look things over? After all, Marshal, we don't even know how they died. Might be a job for the law.'

'Yeah, yeah. You could be right. You get along there and I'll follow when I've seen my deputy.'

The words were as forced as was the expression of dutiful concern. Larry Smith watched the two men leave with a heavy frown on his face. They walked their horses down the street towards the home of the doctor. The marshal grabbed his hat and hurried across to the saloon. His new deputy was leaning against the bar with a glass of beer in his hand.

Jack Shields was a large man, middle-aged and with a dark, heavy face. He looked tough and folks were careful to treat him with respect.

The marshal moved to his side, looked enviously at the beer, and then glanced round to make sure that nobody else was near enough to overhear.

'That Donovan fella is back in town,' he whispered urgently. 'Didn't you tell them two chowheads that I wanted him dead?'

'Sure did, boss. They trailed him and the young fella outa here. I saw them go myself. What's gone wrong?'

The marshal told him and the large man wiped his mouth noisily.

'So what do we do now?' he asked.

'I gotta go along to the doc's place and look busy,' Larry Smith said uncertainly. 'This thing could blow up in our faces. They've found two bodies,

120

there should have been three. Somethin' just doesn't figure. You ride out to the cabin and see what the hell Ted and Chris are playin' at.'

'It's near dark,' the deputy protested.

Larry Smith was not in the mood to be sympathetic.

'You know the way,' he said bluntly, 'and it's only a two- or three-hour ride.'

The marshal turned abruptly on his heel and left the saloon. He walked down the street to the doctor's house. A horse was hitched to the rail but the two bags of bones were missing. He bit his lip and knocked at the partly open door.

The mayor was already there. Word had got around while the marshal was in the saloon. The mortician had arrived with ghoulish eagerness and Lawyer Roberts had just entered in front of the marshal. They all gathered round a plain wooden table in the surgery where Doc Mason was already emptying out the bones and pieces of cloth from one of the blankets. His wife lowered the central lamp a little and brought another one in to the room. She placed it in front of a mirror and then went off to make some coffee for the gathering throng of notables.

Doctor Mason was a short man, inclined to stoutness and stooped. His face was gentle and his myopic eyes were aided by thick, silver-framed glasses. He picked over the bones and laid them out in some order. His hands trembled a little as he did so, and he put the scraps of clothing on one side for a time.

'Well, this is the body of a woman,' he said softly. 'Gettin' on in years, judgin' by the teeth. She'd be about the height of Emma here.'

He nodded towards the door through which his wife had just left.

'The clothes don't tell us a lot,' he went on. 'There's no colour left, and no labels. No rings on the hands, and these scraps of hair are grey. Let's have a look at the other one.'

He laid out the next pile of bones

into some sort of order.

'Well, it's a man. The bulge above the eyes tells us that. The teeth are good but a few are missing. I think . . . ' The doctor stopped in mid-sentence and stood frozen for a moment. It was the mayor who nudged his arm.

'Go on, man,' he urged, 'What do you think?'

Doc Mason picked up one of the skeleton arms and examined the hand. There was still a little flesh attached to the fingers, but it was mixed with sand and formed an ugly mass.

'There are two fingers missin' on the right hand,' the medical man whispered in an anxious voice, 'and the left eye socket shows signs of damage. I've got a feelin' that when I look at the left leg, there'll be an old wound there that made him limp. Broken bone.'

'My God!' the mayor gasped. 'You're tellin' us that it's Tom Wallace and Betty.'

'I'm afraid so.'

Lawyer Roberts looked from one

man to the other. 'So how did they die?' he asked anxiously.

The doctor's hands were trembling badly now as he pointed to fractures in some of the bones.

'They was shot,' he said.

They all looked at Marshal Larry Smith. He was pale and his lips moved silently for a moment until he recovered enough to confront Hank Donovan with something of his newly acquired authority.

'How come you were out at Rossiter Creek?' he asked.

'I'm an engineer for a copper-minin' company,' the large man explained patiently. 'I wanted to check the water there for traces of metal. So I rode out and we was makin' camp for the night when I noticed the disturbed ground. There was a bit of cloth on the surface, so we started digging.'

Larry Smith was about to say something else when he suddenly realized that somebody was missing. The young stranger was not in the surgery.

'And who is this fella who was with you?' he asked in an effort to sound as though he was in command of the situation.

'I don't rightly know,' Hank said in a casual voice, 'but he was anxious to earn a few dollars by escortin' a fat old rube like me on a few days out in the wild. I sure don't fancy workin' alone but the company won't spend more than they need.'

It was the banker who put in the next question.

'Did you find any?' he asked eagerly.

'Any what?'

'Traces of copper.'

Hank Donovan bit back a smile. The prospect of making money was quickly overcoming the loss of a prominent citizen and his wife.

'Too early to say,' he told them. 'I've got to check on the water when I get a chance.'

The mayor brought their attention back to the skeletons on the table.

'We've got ourselves a killin' here,' he

said grimly. 'Tom and Betty were friends of mine. They was fine Southern folk, and they've been killed. What happened to their rig and all their belongings? Any sign?'

'No sign of anythin' like that,' Hank Donovan told him. 'There hadn't been a horse near the creek for weeks, I figure. Are we talkin' about the former owner of the hotel I'm stayin' at?'

He was eagerly assured that he had the right of it.

'I still can't figure out why they ever left town,' Lawyer Roberts said sourly. 'And I certainly can't understand them sellin' the place to Ralph Loman. It don't make sense. Loman ain't got a dime to his name.'

The mayor looked at his cousin Larry. 'What are you figurin' on doing, lad?' he asked.

'I'll ride out there tomorrow and scout around. He must have met up with some wild fellas who just took him for an easy mark. They'll be long gone to the other end of the territory by now.'

There was a nodding of heads as the town leaders filed back in to the other room where coffee and something stronger was waiting for them. The mayor took Hank Donovan by the arm.

'Don't go yet, Mr Donovan,' he said quietly. 'Take a drink with us. After all, if it hadn't been for you, we'd never have known about this tragedy.'

He ignored the silver coffee-pot and poured the big man a measure of the doctor's best whiskey. The others were all in general conversation and not likely to overhear any private words the two men might have.

'Suppose you tell me exactly what you're doin' in town, Mr Donovan,' the mayor suggested quietly. 'I reckon you know as much about the copper minin' business as my horse's ass.'

'You're a suspicious man, Mr Mayor.'

'My ma didn't have no stupid children, fella. If she had, they'd have been marshals of this town. Not the mayor. You were here durin' our celebration of the President's birthday. I saw you watchin' everythin' that went on. You makin' a report back to them Yankees in Washington?'

Hank Donovan smiled and took a sip from his glass.

'When you talk of the president, I take it that you don't mean President Arthur or the late Abe Lincoln?' he mused.

'I sure as hell don't. I mean Jefferson Davis.'

Hank nodded. 'Well, you may rest assured. I won't be tellin' tales to Washington about that event.'

'So what's your real business here?'

Hank Donovan made a decision and his eyes did a quick sweep of the room.

'I'm lookin' for a killer,' he said quietly. 'And I reckon he's in this buildin' right now.'

9

Mayor Smith had an office above his grain-store. The place smelled sweetly of the products he sold and the room was airy with the windows open to let in the cooling air of the night.

He poured out a drink for his guest as the two men sat facing each other across the desk.

'Suppose you tell me your story, Mr Donovan,' the First Citizen invited in an uncertain voice.

The other man pulled out a sheet of paper that identified him. It said more than the simple display of a badge. After it had been read, he told the mayor what he needed to know of events. His tale was followed by a long silence as the two men sipped the good imported whiskey.

'And you apparently don't think I'm the man you're lookin' for,' the mayor said at last, in a quiet voice. 'I suppose that's at least a compliment.'

'I know your background, Mr Mayor. You were too old to be in the war, so you would not have been in contact with this fella Bedser. We also know that you were here before most of the other folk. You were the real founder of this haven for Johnny Rebs. And I reckon as how you don't want to be the victim of a couple of Yankee thieves and killers any more than any decent fella would.'

The mayor nodded vigorously.

'I thought this Bedser rogue was the genuine piece of goods,' he said. 'He came here and told a story of havin' been wounded and havin' married a widow woman with a small boy. He said that his home was destroyed by the Yankees and that he wanted to get as far away from them as possible. He had it all, Marshal. The accent, the old uniforms, a sabre that was presented by the men of his regiment. And he sure as hell could tell a good tale over a few drinks. He took us in like we was a bunch of drunken cowpokes.'

'Well, his accomplice is still here, and he's the dangerous one. I reckon that he had Bedser and his wife killed in case they started talking. Then he sent two fellas to kill me and the young lad who was with me.'

The mayor shook his head in wonderment.

'Then he knows who you are?' he asked.

'I don't think so, but I'm a stranger and that makes him nervous. I reckon your new marshal was told to make sure that I didn't cause trouble. My room has been searched but I had some copper-minin' stuff there. It might not have convinced him, and it sure didn't convince you, Mr Mayor.'

They both laughed and the mayor poured another drink. 'How can I help?' he asked.

'Tell me about the folk who arrived here in the early days. The ones who brought money with them.'

Davy Smith scratched the side of his face.

'Well, Lawyer Roberts weren't short of a dollar or two. He set up here and said he'd been invalided outa the Confederate Army because of fever. He's never been short of money. Comes from Virginia and the accent is right enough.'

He took a sip of whiskey and frowned thoughtfully.

'Judge O'Conner came with his wife and kids at about the same time. He weren't a judge then; just another lawyer. But he was a fair-minded fella and we elected him. He sure had plenty of cash money from the first day. Came from up near Richmond, so he said. Then there was the money-lendin' fella. His name's Moorcroft and he ain't just the manager of the bank. He's what they calls a director. Got shares in the business. And there ain't no shortage of money where he's concerned, I can tell you.'

He paused again for a moment as he took stock.

'Then we got the two saloon-owners. They both came here with money. The Southern Star had another name in them days but Grant Withers soon changed it. He was with the Third Texas Cavalry and wounded out. His saloon back home was burned down and his family killed by Yankee cannon fire. The Texas Belle was built from scratch a coupla years after the war. Lou Gorman owns it and he came to town with a few fancy women and that ugly wife of his. He sure had money and I never did hear tell what he did in the war. Somebody said he'd been a prisoner up at Elmira, and that he served with General Hood.'

Mayor Smith took another sip and thought deeply for a while.

'There must be five or six of the storekeepers who had ready cash when they came here. Luc Delavalle set up the gun-store, and that took cash. And old Dick Barron had the hardware store up and runnin' pretty fast. Mind you, he always over-charged folk, but it took money to get started. There would be another dozen or so fellas of the right age who might fill the bill, Marshal. And it all happened a hell of a long time ago.'

'Yes. Tell me, did Bedser ever drop his cover for a moment? Did he ever say anythin' unusual or was there any special person in town he seemed to know better than the rest of you?'

The mayor shook his head.

'Not that I recall,' he said. 'After all, he had wounds, and the right accent. Even loaned me a copy of Hardee's *Tactics* at one time. He had a fine library of Southern books.' He sighed. 'And I got took in by a Yankee. It's the damnedest thing.'

He shook his head sadly and then brightened up a little.

'But you're here now, Marshal,' he said a little more cheerfully, 'and I reckon you'll soon get a line on this other fella. If you tie in our new lawman with him, cousin or no cousin, I'll have young Larry behind bars before he can spit.'

Marshal Donovan twirled his drink around the glass slowly.

'The trouble is that I got no backing,' he said. 'The fellas in Washington reopened this business when Ralph Loman started askin' questions. It's an old case, and they ain't keen on spendin' money, I reckon. So I got no help. And this is one of them times when I can't rely on the local lawman. Tell me about Loman.'

The mayor pulled a face.

'A real nobody,' he said. 'He never had money of his own and always worked for Major Wallace as hotel manager. It's funny, but I still think of him as Major Wallace. Years of habit, I guess. Ralph Loman's the sorta fella who wouldn't pick a fight with a dead jackrabbit. Rubs his hands together and ducks his head like some wishy-washy waiter in them hotels back East. I heard tell that he was a medical orderly with Dreaux's Battalion from Louisiana. That's why he helped with that dyin' freight-hauler after Cousin Larry did his fancy shootin' a coupla months back.'

Hank Donovan stood up and stretched himself wearily.

'Well, I guess you've helped me all you can, Mr Mayor,' he said, 'and I'm surely grateful. Let's keep all this between ourselves for now. If your cousin Larry doesn't give me a lead by contactin' some fella in town in too obvious a way, I reckon there ain't a lot that can be done after all these years.'

'I'll keep a watch on him too,' the mayor said eagerly. 'I wish we'd never been saddled with Larry. I think I'll go talk to Matt and see if he'll take on the job again. He was a man who could be trusted. What about this young fella you've got?'

'Oh, he ain't no lawman. I gave him a few dollars to ride with me. He had a gun and seemed willin' enough. But he's lookin' for some sort of steady work and I don't want to get him involved in my business. It ain't fair on the lad.'

'Well, the ranches will be lookin' for hands in the next few weeks. The drives to the railhead will be startin' soon. I'll put in a word for him, if you like.'

'I'd be obliged. He seems a steady sort of fella.'

*   *   *

The steady sort of fella was following the new deputy marshal. The moon shone fitfully behind fleeting cloud. The air was noisy with the buzz of insects and a whistling wind. Following a man was not easy but his quarry had to move slowly over the rough ground.

Hank Donovan had watched the marshal of Defiance cross to the Southern Star saloon. He had seen the new deputy marshal come out and go off to saddle his horse. A word to Bill Danvers had been enough. The young man knew what was required and had tightened the girth on his mount. When the newly appointed deputy left town, he was not far behind.

It took more than two hours to reach a small butte that stood out against the dark sky with its scudding clouds and occasional glimpse of the moon. The deputy marshal rode round the edge of the barren rock to where a small cabin was built against the sandstone. There was a glimmer of light from the only window and a corral was nearby.

The visitor dismounted and called to whoever was in the cabin. Bill Danvers was well behind. He got down from his own horse and moved forward on foot. He could see things more plainly as the moon came out to help. The cabin was of rough timber. There was no stove-pipe and the remains of a fire near the closed door still smouldered. There seemed to be three or four horses in the corral, and Bill could hear the sound of water trickling down from the rocks somewhere in the darkness. He crept forward and could hear voices.

He lay on his stomach behind a clump of cactus and watched patiently to see what would happen next.

Nothing did, but after another hour, the deputy marshal came out, unsaddled his horse and led it into the corral to join the others. He went back into the cabin and the light was doused shortly after.

Bill Danvers went back to where his own mount was tethered. He did not know what to do next. Everything was puzzling him. He wanted justice for his murdered mother, and these men seemed to be part of whatever had caused her death. He felt that the federal marshal was using him for his own ends, but that did not matter. When Hank Donovan found out who was behind it all, Bill would make sure that he got to the killer first. Crooked lawyers and bought judges could let a rich, guilty man go free. But Bill would make sure that his mother was avenged.

He sat by his horse, his head resting on a rock still warm from the sun. He dozed occasionally. His thoughts went back to his boyhood and to Tom Wallace. The old rogue had been a good parent, and Bill always thought of him as a father. He was likeable, and good to Bill's mother. It was his money that had helped Bill establish his own place so that he could marry and settle down.

Tom Wallace had always been a Confederate officer to the little boy who grew up on his stories of battles and the glory of the South. The young man smiled grimly. Tom had not deserved killing, and Bill had already made up his mind that everyone involved would be brought to account.

He mused on his own situation. Defiance had once been his home. He had gone to school there, sang at the meeting-house, and been treated by Doc Mason until his mother sent him off to live with her folks up on the Gila. Nobody in Defiance knew him any more. A boy had left and a man came back. Time had moved so quickly and had changed so much.

He did not know what woke him. It was a moment of alarm and his hand went for the gun at his waist. He listened carefully but only the noises of the night came to his ear. Then he heard it again. It was what had woken him: the noise of hoofs on the hard ground.

He silently cursed as he rose to his feet and looked around in the darkness. The moon was low now, and there was a hint of dawn above the hills. His own horse raised its head and let out a little whinny. Bill put a hand over its nose and the animal fell silent again.

Then he saw them. Two horses were coming towards him out of the night. They passed by just a few yards away, moving quite slowly, saddled and with loose stirrups flapping against their flanks. They were heading straight for the butte and he watched them disappear again into the darkness.

Bill ran after the animals. He saw them pass the darkened cabin and stop at the fence of the corral. The horses already there came over to nuzzle them and the newly arrived animals seemed suddenly contented. They were the two horses Hank Donovan had turned loose after their riders had been killed at Rossiter Creek.

A light went on in the cabin and Bill ducked down between the bushes. The door opened noisily and three men came out with guns in their hands. The sky was now lightening enough to make out the figure of the deputy marshal. The other two were older men, heavy and unshaven. One of them carried a lantern and held it up to inspect the two horses.

'Ted and Chris ain't comin' back,' one of the men grated as he ran a hand down the flanks of the animals to see how much they were sweating. 'I reckon as how they've gotten themselves caught or killed.'

A few other words were exchanged in lower voices and Bill could not make out what was said. He watched the men unsaddling the animals and leading them in to the corral. They returned to the cabin and the door closed behind them. Bill crept back to where his horse was chewing the coarse grass and blinking its eyes in the dawn.

The young man sat debating his next move. He now had no doubts that the three men at the cabin were part of the conspiracy that had led to the deaths of his mother and stepfather. But there were three of them there, and the deputy would be an experienced gun. Bill looked towards the butte and cursed his own lack of decision. He would have given a lot to know what was going on in the cabin.

There were three worried men back there. Jack Shields took charge of things, and while one relit the fire to prepare a meal, the deputy told the older of the two what they had better do next.

'I reckon as how we're gonna need all the guns we can get back in Defiance,' he said thoughtfully. 'Larry Smith expects four of you to ride in and take over. I'd better ride over to Cohuanga and get hold of the Pearson boys. They've worked with us before and we sure as hell need them now.'

'And do we wait here for you?'

Jack Shields thought about it for a moment.

'No,' he said. 'I guess it would be better if you rode into town. Larry will be wonderin' what the hell's happened if he don't get some word from me. You can let him know that them two strangers have killed Ted and Chris for certain sure. And tell him that I'm bringin' the Pearsons into town as fast as I can. It's a good two days' journey, so he'll just have to be patient. In the meantime, maybe you and Phil can take care of them two strangers.'

He rode away from the butte an hour later and Bill Danvers was almost taken by surprise when the deputy passed by at a steady pace towards the north. Bill stroked his chin thoughtfully. The deputy marshal was riding away from town, and that did not seem to make sense. There was one helpful thing about it though. It only left two men at the cabin. And Bill Danvers was happier with the reduced odds.

10

Bill Danvers took his Winchester from the saddle holster and checked that it held a full load. He moved silently through the tall grasses towards the butte until he was in sight of the roof of the cabin. There was smoke from the fire near the door. A coffee-pot stood by it and he could smell bacon.

The door was closed and he edged nearer, keeping low amid the grass and scrub. He came within twenty feet of the place and laid himself flat with the rifle thrust out in front of him. He did not want to take any risks by playing the hero, but he hesitated about shooting unarmed or unwary folk. His basic instinct was to fight fair. But then he remembered his mother, and his mouth hardened as he waited to see what would happen. He was still outnumbered and his enemies were professional gunslingers.

He could hear voices after a while. The door opened and a hand appeared with an enamel cup that shot a jet of cold coffee into the open air. The door slammed shut again and the conversation continued. Bill was getting cramp, but he hesitated to move in case the nearby horses caught wind or sight of him and made a noise.

Then the door opened again and the two men emerged. They wore their guns and one carried a Winchester. After closing the door carefully behind them and moving the coffee-pot away from the dying fire, they went to the corral. Their saddles were lying over the top rail and they took them down. Bill watched as they wiped off the dust. It was obvious that they were leaving and he levelled the carbine at the one who was opening the gate.

The shot made the horses rear and scamper wildly round the corral. The man at the gate stumbled for a moment and then slumped to the ground. The gate started to swing shut again but his body stopped it closing all the way. His companion turned round in bewilderment and then made a bolt for the cabin. He slammed the door behind him and Bill could see him peering fearfully through the window. He loosed off another shot and the man ducked as splinters flew from the woodwork by his head.

Bill Danvers fed two more cartridges into the Winchester and cocked it again. He waited patiently to see what happened. The explosion took him by surprise. He jumped instinctively as a charge of buckshot slashed at the bushes around him. He hugged the earth as another charge shivered a clump of mesquite a little to his right.

Something was stinging his face and he brushed a slightly shaky hand across his cheek. He was bleeding. Some of the shot had caught him without doing any real damage. He levelled the gun and aimed carefully at the window. There was no movement from inside the cabin.

Bill glanced around, looking for inspiration. He could not get at the horses to free them and leave his enemy on foot. The gate of the corral was ajar but they would not cross the body of the man lying in the opening. He could not move over the ground without another blast from the shotgun at close range. Bill bit his lip anxiously. He did not want to leave the place with the job unfinished.

There was another possibility and he decided to try it. He crawled backwards until he was out of range and sight of the cabin. He got to his feet and ran towards the rocky wall of the butte. It was easy enough to edge along the base through the bushes and cactus-groups that sent clouds of dust into the air as he moved. There was no window in the side of the cabin and he was able to approach it without being seen. He stopped at the rough wooden wall and put his hand on the dry timbers. They would burn well.

Bill began to pile up all the loose bits

148

of twig and dry grasses he could find. Broken branches and dead mesquite were pushed against the cabin wall. He took the vesta box from his shirt and lit the pile of rubbish. It needed several attempts but the dry foliage caught at last and flames began to leap up at the side of the little building.

Bill Danvers quietly withdrew and crawled carefully to his original position where he could watch the door of the place. He could see the flames from where he was. There was little smoke. The kindling was too dry for that. He smiled grimly as he lay in wait.

The door suddenly burst open and a man came stumbling out of the cabin. He dropped on his belly as he crossed the threshold and fired wildly with a shotgun. The blast was well away from where Bill lay hidden, but it kept him under cover. Another charge of shot followed and the young man could hear several of the pellets tearing through the bushes near his head. He looked up, knowing that his opponent had emptied the gun. The man was running towards the corral, drawing a revolver as he dragged at the gate and edged round the body of the dead man.

Bill jumped to his feet. He felt more confident now and unholstered his own .44.

'I'm over here, fella!' he shouted.

His opponent turned and levelled the Colt. He fired a single shot at extreme range and Bill winced as a sudden pain tore across the calf of his left leg. He pulled the trigger of his own gun but missed. He knew where his shot had gone. One of the saddles on the rail shuddered for a moment. Bill recocked the gun and levelled it carefully. Before he could pull the trigger, another shot hit the ground near his foot and he instinctively jumped backwards. He cursed himself and tried to aim again.

His opponent was now partly sheltered by the horses as they milled around. His hand was on the headband of a small roan when Bill fired again. The hand clutched at the mane as the man tried to stay upright. He seemed to be almost stroking the animal as he began to slide to the ground. The horse swung round, knocking the man flat as it went to join the other animals. The gunslinger tried to get to his feet again and then took a final tumble. The horses looked at him with mild interest and then resumed their chewing at the dry grass.

Bill checked that both men were dead. Then he entered the small cabin to look around. It was partly filled with smoke which hung in oily layers. The place was clean enough, with a few stools and a large table of rough planks. There were some bunks and a few clothes hung on the wooden walls. There was nothing of interest and the young man went thankfully back to the fresh air.

He crossed to the corral and moved the body that partly blocked the gate. He pulled the other man out of the corral as well and left them lying side by side. With the gate wide open, the animals could move about as they willed. He did think about taking them back to town, but the brands seemed to have been changed in a very rough way, and he decided to leave them.

There was little money in the pockets of the two corpses. Nothing more than three and a half dollars in all. Neither had a watch although the man he had shot first carried a large pouch of tobacco and a corn-cob pipe. Bill left them and went back to his horse.

He suddenly realized that he was limping slightly and that his left boot seemed to be full of liquid. The wound in his calf was numb but blood had trickled down his leg and his toes were sticky with it. He sat on the ground as his horse watched. The boot came off easily and he rolled up his pants to get a better look at the injury. It was a deep gouge but there was no bullet. He tied a bandanna around it and wiped out the boot with some dry grass. It felt comfortable enough but he would need to visit a doctor when he got to Defiance.

He mounted his horse and rode slowly back to town.

11

Bill Danvers arrived back in Defiance at about the time the children were going to the schoolhouse. They looked at him without interest even though he nodded a greeting to some of the prettier mothers. The sky was cloudy and the town quiet so early in the day. Bill's calf was hurting after the ride and with the tight bandage he had wound round it.

His first call would be to the Beauregard hotel and then he would have to visit Doctor Mason. He had slept the night on the range, resting his leg and trying to pick out some of the pellets from his face and neck. The dead men had been left unburied, but their ammunition was in Bill's saddle-bags. He had left their guns but collected the few dollars they carried.

Hank Donovan had just finished breakfast and his face lit up when the young man put in an appearance. He listened to the tale with deep interest and congratulated him on how he had acted.

'I reckon that deputy has gone off to round up some more fellers to help him and Larry Smith,' he mused. 'It was as well you killed them two. This town could be in for trouble. We'd better get you to the doctor and have that leg fixed. And your face could do with some patchin' up while he's at it. You look like some fella what's got the pox.'

He led the way jovially along the street to Doc Mason's house. The medical man was at home and hurried them into the surgery while his wife went off to heat some water. Doc Mason looked at the leg carefully. His glasses rested on the edge of his nose as he probed the flesh round the wound with gentle fingers.

'Well, it ain't nothin' bad,' he said softly, 'but it surely needs a good clean and a few stitches. You was one lucky fella that you got off so lightly.'

The doctor went over to a cupboard and took out his heavy oak instrument-case. He laid it on the table and opened it up with a certain air of pride. The instruments gleamed cleanly and Bill Danvers looked a little scared at what he saw. There was a hammer, long knives that were razor-sharp, a large saw, and a collection of ugly probes. He swallowed noisily while Hank Donovan looked on complacently.

'Now, I can give you some ether for this, lad,' the doctor said quietly, 'but you'll be as sick as a greedy schoolkid afterwards. It's best if I just tend you as fast as I can. It'll hurt a bit but I reckon it's easier in the end. All I gotta do is clean up the wound, cut away some tissue, and then sew you up as neat as a new suit of clothes.'

Bill sighed. 'Go ahead, Doc,' he said as firmly as he could. 'I guess I can take it.'

Doc Mason nodded and chose some of the instruments. His wife entered with a jug of boiling water, and while

Hank Donovan looked on, the job began.

The medical man's hands were swift and sure. He was gentle and caring as he worked. Bill groaned and twitched a few times, but the worst was soon over and he was looking at a neatly bandaged leg. The doctor patted him on the arm.

'I'll take out the stitches in a few days and you'll be as bright as a new one-dollar bill.'

He looked at the two men and took off his glasses.

'I suppose it ain't my business, but is this a job for the town marshal?' he asked.

Bill hesitated for a moment and Hank Donovan took over.

'I don't think my young friend here wants to bother the law with a private matter that took place away from town,' he said smoothly. 'I reckon the new marshal's got enough on his hands.'

Doctor Mason nodded. 'That could well be the best thing,' he agreed. 'And as a medical fella, it ain't my business to go tellin' tales. Which of you is footin' the bill, might I ask?'

Mrs Mason dealt with matters like that. Bill went into the next room to pay her while the doctor washed the instruments in the rest of the hot water. He laid them lovingly in the wooden case while Donovan stood at his side.

'They're sure a murderous collection,' the federal marshal said.

'They are indeed,' Wally Mason agreed enthusiastically. 'The sharpest you'll ever find and made by one of the best firms. I ain't never come across anythin' better.'

'I see they're British,' Donovan said as the case was put back in the cupboard.

'Yes. Place is the name. From Manchester. They supplied both armies durin' the war. Strictly neutral when it came to makin' money they were.'

The two men laughed and passed through to the other room where a whiskey-bottle waited.

Hank Donovan and Bill Danvers walked slowly back to the hotel. They passed the jailhouse where Larry Smith sat on the stoop. He looked at them suspiciously but said nothing. Hank told the young man about the arrangements that were being made to give a proper burial to the collection of bones they had found. The preacher had already been informed and the mortician was fixing up a special casket. Bill thanked the federal man while they sat together in cane chairs on the stoop of the hotel. Marshal Smith could see them from where he was as he waited impatiently for the return of his deputy and the men he would bring.

'What happens next?' Bill Danvers asked the man at his side.

'Well, now as to that, young fella, I don't pretend to know.'

The federal marshal looked towards the jailhouse where the stoop was now empty.

'I think I savvy who's behind all this, but I ain't sure. That marshal fella knows and I figure more men are bein' brought into town to control things and keep the lid on it all. I reckon we simply have to wait and see. There's just two of us, and only the devil knows how many there are of them. Let's go take a drink. I need cheerin' up.'

★   ★   ★

Ralph Loman was behind his desk. A short-barrelled Colt lay in front of him and the door was locked. The shutters were drawn across the window and an oil-lamp lit the place. The hotel owner was afraid. He had felt safe when Hank Donovan was about, but he had seen him cross the street to the Southern Star and now felt isolated and vulnerable. He tried to concentrate on a newspaper, but his attention wandered as he worried about the future.

The hard rap on the door made him jump and reach out for the pistol.

'Who is it?' he asked fearfully.

'The marshal.'

He got up and admitted Larry Smith. The lawman watched as he carefully bolted the door again.

'You sure as hell is one scared man,' he said with a broad grin.

'I got reason to be.'

'Ain't that the truth? Well, I think it's time I helped you out, fella. But a good deed cuts both ways, don't it?'

The lawman had seated himself comfortably opposite the desk and watched as Ralph Loman went back to his own chair.

'What do you mean by that?' the little man asked. 'How can I help you? And more to the point, how can you help me?'

'Well, now, I need to know about folks what comes to my town and causes trouble. This Donovan fella, for example. Who in hell is he?'

Ralph Loman shrugged. 'Some sort of copperminin' engineer, is what he said,' he whined. 'I don't go pryin' into the affairs of my guests. That wouldn' be right.'

'Sure wouldn't. But I don't reckon him for that. He's too nosy by far. And this young fella what's goin' round with him. What do you figure to him?'

'I've no idea. Just some outa-work cowpoke, I guess.'

'You ain't a lotta help, fella. I was hopin' we could strike a deal.'

'What — what sorta deal, Marshal?'

'I happen to know how you got hold of this place. It cost you five dollars, so they tell me.'

Ralph nearly slipped out of the chair.

'How the hell did you . . . ?'

'I'm a lawman and certain folks talk to me. Y'see, the man we knew as Major Wallace spoke to somebody else before he left town. And that somebody pulls one hell of a lotta weight in Defiance. Right now that friend of mine's runnin' scared in case Wallace, or whatever his name really is, said somethin' to you. Somethin' about havin' a partner at one time.'

'Major Wallace told me nothin' at all, Marshal,' the hotel owner whined. 'I just found out that he wasn't one of us and I put on some pressure. He sold out to me and took himself and his wife outa town. I didn't even know someone else was involved until Marshal Don . . . '

He suddenly realized what he had said, or was on the verge of saying. The lawman stood up and leaned over the desk. He towered above the little man and his face was menacing.

'I reckon as how you'd better tell me the whole tale, fella,' he said in a threatening voice.

'I — I . . . ' Ralph Loman was sweating and his face paled as he cowered in his chair.

'Lookit, Ralphy boy,' the marshal said grimly. 'If I go on to the street and tell folk that you paid five dollars to a Yankee thief to get this hotel, they'll be real sore. They lynched that wagon fella just 'cos he worked with a Yankee. What the hell do you think they'd do to one of their own who didn't tell them he was harbourin' a Bluebelly who was laughin' up his sleeve at us? They'd sure as hell have you swingin' in no time.'

'What exactly do you want?' The words came out with difficulty through terrified lips.

'I want this place. You take yourself to one of them lawyer fellas and make out a deed of sale. Then you pack your bags and get the hell outa my town. If you don't, one of two things will happen. Either the folks round here will kill you, or I will.'

Ralph Loman nodded his head wildly.

'I'll go,' he promised. 'I'll do exactly as you say.'

Larry Smith grinned and tapped the little man on the cheek.

'You're one wise fella, Ralph,' he said. 'Now, suppose you tell me all about this marshal you mentioned. And don't even think of givin' me any lies.'

Ralph Loman was not a hero and he told all that he knew about Hank Donovan. The lawman listened quietly, just nodding his head occasionally. The story completed, the hotel-owner drew out a large bandanna and wiped his face.

'You sure have been keepin' secrets.' The marshal grinned. 'Well, it's all over now. You come along to the jailhouse this afternoon with that bill of sale and all your worries are over. You hitch your horse to a surrey and go where the hell you fancy.'

Ralph Loman's face clouded.

'Major Wallace and his wife went off in a surrey,' he said fearfully. 'And we all know what happened to him. I'll use the stage. It's due in town on Thursday.'

The marshal thought about it for a moment.

'I reckon that'll do,' he said. 'Just tell your hired help that I'll be ownin' this place from tomorrow. And one more thing. Don't talk no more to Donovan. I got fellas comin' in to town who wouldn't take too kindly to that.'

He tapped the hotel-owner on the side of the face again in a friendly gesture and left the room. Ralph slumped in his chair and wept.

★   ★   ★

A puzzled Lawyer Roberts had his clerk write out a bill of sale as Ralph Loman required. No money was mentioned and he assumed that cash was paid or that some instalment deal had been made. The fact that the new owner was Marshal Smith intrigued the legal man and he would have liked to talk to the mayor or the bank manager. Only his sense of duty prevented it and he stayed silent and wary.

The stage arrived as usual on Thursday noon. A couple of passengers got off while the mail and a little freight was unloaded. No passengers boarded it, and after time for a meal and a change of horses, it took off again amid a cloud of reddish dust.

Marshal Smith walked cheerfully along to the Wells Fargo office to collect his official mail. He then sat contentedly on the jailhouse stoop reading it.

It was early afternoon when the odd-job lad from the Beauregard hotel came running down the street. He stopped at the rail of the jailhouse and waved his arms wildly as he tried to tell the marshal what had happened.

Ralph Loman had killed himself.

12

The bedroom was a large one that overlooked the back of the hotel. It was well furnished with quality pieces from back East and had a thick Turkey carpet on the floor. Three leather cases lay by the wardrobe with a topcoat lying across them. The four men stood in silence as they looked at the body while the ticking of the wall clock seemed loud in the quiet room.

Doctor Mason bent over the chair by the side of the bed. His hands trembled as he viewed the amount of blood and the neatly severed throat of Ralph Loman. A thin, long knife was still in the clutch of the dead man. Ralph Loman had killed himself while sitting upright, his shirt open at the neck and his head fallen forward so that his balding pate shone in the light.

'What sort of knife is that, Doc?'

Marshal Smith asked tautly.

The medical man picked it up in an absent sort of way.

'It's an amputation knife,' he said quietly. 'Just about the best thing you could use in this case.'

'What would he be doin' with a thing like that?' the mayor asked. His face was ashen and he looked as if he was going to sick.

'He was in a medical unit durin' the war,' the doctor murmured. 'I recall some mention of it.'

The mortician said nothing. He was calculating the length of the body and wondering how much he could charge for the funeral arrangements.

'Well, I figure as how we have to talk about this, Larry,' the mayor said grimly. 'I'll leave the details here to you two fellas while the marshal and me sort out a few things. We'll go along to my office.'

He led the way from the room and out of the hotel. His cousin followed meekly and neither man noticed that

Hank Donovan was standing among the other curious folk as they passed through the lobby.

The mayor did not offer the marshal a drink. His colour had gone back to normal and he waved his cousin to a chair with something of his old authority.

'You got some explainin' to do, fella,' he said angrily. 'I hear tell that Ralph Loman sold you the hotel and was clearin' outa town. So tell me it ain't true.'

Larry grinned. He felt that he had the situation under control.

'Me and Loman had an arrangement,' he said cheerfully. 'He'd been coverin' up for a Yankee thief who'd taken you folks in well and truly. I decided to play him at his own game. Marshallin' ain't never gonna make a fella rich. So I did a deal for the hotel and told him to leave Defiance. That's why his bags was all packed back there.'

'And that left him nothin' at all.' The mayor spat out the words in disgust.

170

'He'd been a nobody all his life, and when he did get hitched on to somethin' good, along you come and ruin it for him. No wonder he cut his throat.'

'Well now, Cousin Davy, are you sympathizin' with the fella?'

'No, damme, I ain't. But I can see what it did to him. So now you own the hotel. You're gettin' to be one mighty important fella yourself, Larry. You could be gettin' too big for your own good.'

The mayor looked hard at his cousin and then a slow smile lit his face.

'But you got yourself a problem, young man,' he said softly. 'Whoever you're workin' for is one pretty desperate fella right now. He's got to trust you not to tell us his name. And that makes you a real candidate for the preacher. Have you thought about that?'

Larry Smith tightened his mouth but managed to grin in an effort to show that he was not worried.

'I can't be done no harm,' he boasted. 'I got more fellas comin' into town in the next day or so. They're gonna be my deputies, and they'll be keepin' law and order better than you ever had it, Cousin Davy.'

The mayor half-rose from his chair in alarm.

'We can't pay for more deputies,' he shouted. 'And the council won't have you appointin' them without their say-so.'

'Oh, yes they will. The only folks that will have to pay them are the folks who want their protection. Saloon-owners and local ranchers will kick in for a start. Lookit, Cousin Davy, we can have Defiance the most law-abidin' town in all the territory, and the richest. We got cowpokes and timber-cutters comin' in every weekend. Then we got them copper-minin' fellas comin' in every three or four weeks. There'll be railroad builders soon. You can be runnin' a safe town for folks to visit. And my deputies will earn their keep by doin' what you and me tells them. How do you like that for an idea?'

The mayor rapped his fingers nervously on the desk.

'You been doin' one hell of a lotta thinking, fella,' he muttered.

'I sure have, and my thinkin' includes you, Cousin Davy.'

The mayor's head jerked up. 'Me?' he asked nervously.

'Sure. I ain't the sorta fella to run a classy hotel. That's more in your line of work. I reckon we can make some arrangement where we both profit. Keep it in the family, so to speak.'

The First Citizen's expression began to soften. He got up and went across for the whiskey bottle and glasses.

'We'll have to play it carefully,' he said slowly. 'There's a federal marshal in town.'

'Donovan. Yeah, I know. He can't find out who the Yankee fella is without my help, and I ain't talkin' us outa all that money that was stole. So he'll eventually get tired and leave us in

173

peace. If he doesn't . . . '

'No!' The mayor's voice was sharp and that of a man in control again. 'You'll bring down the whole Washington caboodle on us if you touch him. Just let him get tired of hangin' around. He's already told me that Washington ain't givin' him much support.'

Larry Smith nodded his agreement. 'And when he goes,' he said, 'our family will control Defiance. There's a lot of money to be made out of it.'

★　★　★

The federal marshal was still in the hotel when the mayor and the town lawman left. He walked slowly up the stairs and stopped at the open door of the bedroom. Doctor Mason was aiding the mortician with the body while an assistant was cleaning up some of the mess. The federal man entered the room and closed the door behind him to keep out the people who had gathered on the landing.

'I ain't sure you should be here,' the mortician said uneasily. He had no wish that folk should witness the rough handling of dead bodies and the lack of respect shown them.

'I got business here,' Hank Donovan said as he took out his badge.

He looked at the bed where the corpse now lay in a laid-out position with the rigor mortis broken. His quick eye took in the furnishings and the knife that now lay on a side table. It was next to an untouched supper tray and he picked it up and weighed it in his hand. There was a copper oil-lamp on the table with a pale shade of frosted glass. He lifted it to smell the wick and check how much oil was left, As he put it down, his foot touched something just under the bed. The marshal bent down to pick up a copy of a Washington Irving book. It had been lying face down and two of the pages were bent inwards and slightly torn. The federal man laid it on the table next to the knife.

'How long has he been dead, Doc?' he asked.

'I suppose some time durin' the night,' the medico said uncertainly. 'He's stiffened up quite a bit so I'd put it down to about midnight. Does it matter?'

'I don't know. Any note?'

'Note?' The other men spoke at almost the same time.

'Yes,' the marshal said patiently. 'When folk kill themselves, they like to leave us a note. They usually feel they gotta justify what they're doin' so that the preacher will look kindly on them.'

The doctor nodded his understanding.

'We haven't found one here,' he said, 'but it could be downstairs, I suppose.'

The federal marshal took one last look round and nodded his thanks. He went back down the stairs and crossed to the Southern Star saloon. Bill Danvers was already there and the lawman joined him for a drink.

'You've heard all about Ralph Loman?' he asked as he raised his glass.

'Yeah, and I don't reckon as how he killed himself,' Bill said grimly.

'Funnily enough, neither do I. There was a book on the floor, and I figure as how he was gonna eat his supper and have a read, all peaceful-like. Then somebody knocked on the door. He dropped the book, didn't have a chance to do much else, and got his throat cut. The oil-lamp went on burnin' all night until the oil ran out and the wick began to char. He was murdered sure as shooting.'

'What happens next?' Bill Danvers asked. 'I still aim to find the fella behind this, and I aim to kill him. You got any objection to that?'

Hank Donovan shrugged. 'I'm here to arrest him and take the fella in for trial. There ain't a lot I can do if you get to him first. And I reckon as how your way will be one hell of a lot better. A trial is a long-winded affair. And if a rich fella has the right friends, it can be real hard to put him away. The law and justice don't walk the same side of the street. I found that out years ago, lad. Just so you don't go murderin' folks, that's all. A gunfight fair and square just ain't my business.'

Hank looked round the saloon and leaned a little closer to his companion.

'Folk round here already know I'm a federal man,' he said cheerfully. 'That won't make me popular, but on the other hand, I reckon it should make me safe. If anythin' happened to me, all hell would break out back in Washington. Them desk fellas would get off their asses for once in their lives. They can't let a federal man get killed without doin' somethin' about it. Even this dumb marshal should know that. But just in case, I reckon I'd better tell you who we're after.'

The young man listened in astonishment as the lawman told him the story quietly and without emotion. When the tale was finished, the two men stood in silence for a while.

'That sure beats anythin' I expected,' Bill said softly.

'Surprised me, but when you think about it, it's likely enough. But, given who it is, you'd better let me take him, son. I'll do it quietly one night when I've made arrangements to get him outa town. If folk think I'm takin' one of their own, I might have trouble. And if they found out who he really is, they'd surely lynch him.'

Bill nodded. 'And what about that deputy I saw headin' north? He's gonna come back here with a gang of some sort. What happens then?'

'I don't know, lad, but just make sure you've got plenty of ammunition.'

13

Jack Shields returned to the town by himself. He rode in quietly one evening just as the sun was setting amid a belt of thick cloud. Nobody seemed to notice as he unsaddled his horse behind the jailhouse and let it drink at the trough. He entered the building by the back door and his boss looked up with relief written plainly on his face.

'Where the hell have you been?' he snapped. 'And where are the others? Things are comin' to a head round here.'

'Ted and Chris is dead. Their horses came back to the cabin while I was there with Phil and Sam.'

Larry Smith bit his lip angrily. 'Have you brought them back with you then?' he asked.

'They're dead as well.'

'Look, fella, this is no time for funny stories . . . '

'I ain't jokin' none, boss. You sent Ted and Chris to deal with them two strangers, and I figure as how they got theirs tryin' to do exactly that. So I told Phil and Sam to come into town and tell you what had happened while I rode out to get the Pearsons. We came back by way of the cabin so that we could rest up there. Phil and Sam were lyin' by the corral. They'd been dead for days.'

Larry Smith tapped his fingers restlessly on the wooden arms of the chair.

'So how many of the Pearson gang are here?' he asked.

'Five. Old Alf himself, one of his sons, and three hired hands. But they saw them bodies and they're surely gonna want plenty out of this deal.'

'Where are they now?'

'I left them about an hour's ride outa town. Seemed the best thing to do. We need to clear this place out and make for points west.'

The marshal looked at him. 'That weren't my original plan,' he said softly, 'but things is changin' fast. I figured on us makin' this town our own and milkin' it for every bent cent. My cousin, the mayor, was gonna help once he saw the sense of it. But it's all changed now and I calculate that we make one big killin' and get the hell out. We'll bring in the Pearson gang, loot the bank, all the stores, and I'll squeeze the last drops outa my particular prize turkey.'

He began to cheer up at the thought.

'But we'll not head west,' he went on. 'We'll head for the border with every horse in town and everythin' we can put across their saddles. It'll be the biggest haul in the territory, and we'll be long gone before anythin' can be done about it. There ain't no guns around here that can take us on.'

He was starting to get enthusiastic at his own genius when another thought occured to him. The marshal stood up and crossed restlessly to the window. He looked out on to the quiet street.

'The two fellas we sent after them

strangers must have been shot by them. But Phil and Sam — that's a different story. That Donovan fella stayed in Defiance. He was with me at the doc's house when we looked at them skeletons. I noticed the young lad had gone missing. I reckon he followed you outa town and you led him to the cabin. He killed Phil and Sam after you left to get the Pearsons.'

Jack Shields had been pouring himself a cup of coffee. He stopped with the pot raised in his hand.

'Phil was kin of mine,' he said. 'I'm gonna kill that young fella.'

'We'll kill both of them. They're workin' together and they're the only two guns in town we have to worry about. But I've got to go on lookin' like a peace officer until we're ready. So have you. Let's just wait a while.'

*　*　*

One man noticed Jack Shields return to Defiance. Hank Donovan missed very little and he saw him go round to the corral. The federal man sat on the hotel stoop, puzzling over why he had arrived alone. He got up from his chair after a while and crossed to the Southern Star saloon. Bill Danvers was eating a meal at one of the small tables. He looked up at the arrival of Hank Donovan.

He was quickly told what had happened, and like Donovan, he wondered why Jack Shields was alone.

'He could have his men encamped somewheres outa town,' he suggested.

'I reckon that's the case,' Donovan agreed, 'and he sure as hell ain't gonna lead us to them. I don't know what this marshal is plannin' to do next, but I reckon as how things are gonna bust wide open at any time.'

Bill put down his fork. 'There's more than one way to skin a polecat,' he said with a grin. 'Suppose I just ask that deputy fella where they are?'

★   ★   ★

The stores were beginning to open and a few people were on the main street. The marshal was standing in front of the jailhouse while his deputy was making coffee. They were both looking forward to the time of pillage that lay ahead. Larry Smith watched idly as a man came round the corner from the corrals. He was leading a horse and stopped outside the Beauregard hotel. It was the young fellow who had been with Donovan. The marshal became suddenly alert.

He watched tautly as the federal man came out and spoke a few words to the horseman. Donovan was pointing along the street and making gestures with his hands as though giving directions. The marshal hurried into the jailhouse.

'Leave the coffee,' he instructed his deputy. 'That young fella is goin' outa town, and he's in cahoots with Donovan again. Get saddled up and follow him. Now's the chance to settle up and then we'll only have one to deal with.'

Jack Shields did not need telling

twice. He put down the tin mug and hurried out of the back door to the corral where his horse was kept.

He was on his way a short time later, following the dusty trail of the young rider. The man was heading south, moving quite slowly and in the direction of a range of low hills edged with trees. The sun grew hotter and the deputy was sucking his lips to get rid of the irritating dryness.

They entered the line of low trees that grew at such a slant that they looked as if they might fall over at any minute. The prevailing wind had determined their growth and the branches brushed against the faces of the riders. Jack Shields lost sight of his quarry. He reined in the horse and listened carefully. There were no animal or bird noises and all that moved seemed to be the endless flies that buzzed around him.

Then he caught a sound almost dead ahead. It was the noise of a horse crashing through the low branches and prickly bushes. Jack Shields drew a sigh of relief and followed the noise slowly and as quietly as he could.

The trees eventually thinned and as he saw the open slopes ahead, the horse came into sight. There was nobody in the saddle.

Jack Shields suppressed a curse. He looked wildly around for signs of life among the trees he was just leaving. A figure stood in front of a wilted sycamore. It was Bill Danvers.

'You'd better get down from that horse, fella,' the young man said in an even voice. 'I don't want to shoot an innocent animal while I'm killin' you.'

Jack Shields looked hard at his opponent. The young fellow carried a gun at his side and his hand was only inches from the butt. The deputy marshal swung his animal round, drawing as he did so. He pulled the horse's head up to give himself more cover and let fly a single shot.

Bill had seen it coming and he dropped to the ground as he also loosed off a single shot. The deputy missed, but Bill's bullet caught the horseman in the heel of his right leg. He let out a yelp of pain and hardly noticed when Bill ran across and grabbed the injured leg. He gave a heave and the deputy was thrown from the saddle to lie writhing among the bushes. His gun had flown from his hand and his horse wandered off a few yards.

Bill Danvers stood over him, a broad grin on his face as he holstered the Colt.

'Well, I reckon as how we can now have a quiet talk,' he said cheerfully. 'I want you to tell me where your gang is hidin' out.'

The deputy sat up and his hands reached down to nurse the damaged heel.

'I got no gang,' he moaned. 'And I was only followin' you because the marshal told me to. My leg's broke, fella. I need a doctor.'

'You surely do, and that's why we're gonna talk. You tell me where those fellas are, and I'll take you back to town. But if you gets all uppity, then I'll just leave you here and go hunt 'em myself. You'll have no horse, no food or water, and one hell of a walk on one good leg. Then there's the coyotes. We got lots of them back home, so I reckon there must be a few round these parts. They smell blood, and a pack of them would sure like to get their teeth into a wounded man who couldn't move no more.'

There was a long silence as Jack Shields thought over his position. Bill Danvers had gone to collect the deputy's animal. He whistled to his own mount and it trotted back to nuzzle the new companion.

'What are you aimin' to do about the fellas you call my gang?' Jack Shields eventually spat out.

'Oh, I'll just ask them not to come in to Defiance. The folks there want to keep it a quiet town.'

'And then you'll come back here for me?'

'Now you're gettin' it.'

'Why not take me with you? I could show you the way.'

'You can tell me the way. And make no mistake, fella. You steer me wrong and you'll never get back to town alive. I'll just leave you here for the coyotes. And the buzzards.'

Jack Shields swallowed his pride and gave accurate details through gritted teeth. He watched the young man mount his horse and ride away, leading the deputy's animal on a long rein.

Bill had not much more than an hour to reach the little creek where the Pearson gang were camped. They were easy to spot as the smoke rose from their cooking-fire. He tethered the two horses behind a mass of bushes and approached carefully. There were five of them, sitting around the flames, talking noisily and drinking from a shared jug of corn mash. They had posted no guard and never noticed him as he grinned his satisfaction and went back to the horses.

★ ★ ★

His report to Marshal Donovan was concise. The older man listened impassively and nodded his head in agreement with the result.

'And you didn't go back for Jack Shields?' he asked when the tale was told.

Bill grinned. 'I don't need to,' he said. 'When he starts thinkin' things over, he'll realize that he's only got about a day's crawl to reach town. He can make it back here with a broken heel. And I don't reckon to be owin' him any favours.'

'I guess not. Sounds like you can use that gun real well.'

'We got rustlers in my part of the world. I usually hit what I aim at, Mr Donovan. What do we do now?'

'Well, I think we'll go see the marshal. He knows by now who I am and he's still posin' as the guardian of law and order. So let's use him.'

Bill pulled a face. 'He's a fella I want

191

to be killing,' he said.

'I won't be arguin' with that when the time comes, lad. But right now we gotta stop them five fellas comin' into town. Let's go help the marshal form a posse.'

★   ★   ★

The mayor sat rather uneasily at his desk. Doc Mason was on his left while the judge sprawled on the other side. Several town worthies sat around, hoping that whiskey would appear. Mayor Smith was too rattled to think about the niceties of hospitality. He threw a cautious look at his cousin and called the meeting to order.

He introduced Marshal Donovan officially for the first time, told nothing of the federal man's mission, and waved a hand to the visitor to state his case. They all looked at him with interest. Larry Smith had a hostile and slightly scared expression. He was even more nervous than his cousin, the mayor.

Things were going wrong, and he knew it. He had seen the young fellow come back to town, but there was no sign of Jack Shields. The marshal had to make a conscious effort to listen to what was happening in the room.

'In the course of my duties,' Hank Donovan said in a slowly modulated official tone, 'I come across certain bits of information that have nothin' to do with the case on which I'm working. I've been told that there are five fellas camped out near a creek less than an hour away from town. They ain't makin' trouble yet, but they've all got records as real bad 'uns. If they decided to come into Defiance and disturb the peace, it sure would be a nuisance. I'm certain we all agree on that.'

They all agreed with an eager nodding of heads. Except for Larry Smith. He had gone a paler shade and his fingers edged towards the butt of his gun.

'So what do you figure on doin' about it, Mr Donovan?' the judge wheezed.

'Well, these fellas may be just passin' through on their way to choir-practice. We can't go arrestin' them and your jailhouse ain't built for that many folks, anyway. If we got a big enough posse together, and I mean big, and rode out there, I figure as how they'd break camp and head for pastures new. They'd know that this town meant business.'

The councillors looked doubtful. There was no sign of any of them setting an example by volunteering.

'Would there be any shooting?' Doc Mason asked.

'Not a chance. If thirty or so fellas suddenly appeared at your campin'-site, would you start shootin' at 'em? I reckon that with the marshal here leadin' them, the posse will scare the hell outa the gang. They'll up stakes all peaceful-like.'

The judge slapped the desk. 'You sure as hell got a smooth way of dealin' with trouble, Marshal,' he croaked. 'I'd go with you if I could ride a horse. I vote we send out a posse this very day.'

It was easier said than done. Eighteen volunteers were finally brave enough to saddle up their mounts and gather round Marshal Smith as he gave them their orders. He was watched by young Bill Danvers who was leading them to their quarry. Marshal Donovan stood in the background with the mayor.

'There ain't gonna be no shootin' in this little shindig,' Larry Smith told them firmly. 'We ride in a tight bunch, and when these fellas see us, they're gonna goin' harin' off like scalded cats. So just remember that you ain't takin' risks if you do as you're told. It won't do no harm to go whoopin' it up and wavin' ropes in the air as soon as we sight them. Our job is just to scare the fellas off.'

That lightened up the spirits of the posse and they rode off a few minutes later. The children cheered them and a few of the women waved bandannas. It made the men feel like heroes going off to battle.

Donovan watched them go and hoped that his judgement was not misplaced.

★ ★ ★

They had ridden for about a quarter of an hour when Larry Smith called a halt. He got down from his mount and went round to its head. He knelt down and ran a hand tenderly over the right fetlock before heaving a sigh of regret.

'She's gone lame,' he said glumly. 'I reckon I'll just have to make it back to Defiance as best I can. Young Bill Danvers here can lead the way, and I guess you don't really need a marshal, anyways. You'll all be back in town in a couple of hours, and I'll buy every one of you a drink at the Southern Star.'

The posse rode off a few minutes later and Larry Smith watched until it was out of sight. Then he remounted and rode at full speed back to town.

14

Hank Donovan watched the posse leave Defiance as he stood at Doc Mason's side. The little group soon split up, and as the medical man moved towards his own house, he felt a firm hand grasping his right arm. The federal marshal smiled at him and the grip tightened.

'I'd like a little talk with you, Doc,' he said cheerfully. 'Let's just go across to the jailhouse where we won't be disturbed.'

'I'm a rather busy man, Marshal — '

'So am I, and right now I figure that you're the one I'm busy about.'

He steered the unresisting man across the street and seated him comfortably in one of the bentwood chairs by the desk.

'I seem to be the only official representative of law and order in town right now,' Donovan said as he took the large swivel-chair of authority. 'You and me has a lot to talk about, Doc. Y'see, I don't reckon as how Marshal Smith will be comin' back to town. And I know that his deputy ain't gonna do no law-enforcement until he can walk one hell of a lot better. And them five gunslingers that them two were bringin' into town, well, they'll soon be headin' for distant parts. So that sorta leaves me in charge. Ain't that cosy?'

'I'm afraid I don't understand what you're gettin' at, Marshal,' the little man said tremulously.

'You've heard the story goin' around town about Major Wallace and how he stole from the Yankees?'

'Of course. Everybody's talkin' about it. And that he had some help doin' it. Somebody right here in Defiance.'

'Exactly.' Donovan nodded agreement. 'And when the folk find out who it was, they'll sure be lynchin' mad, Doc.'

The little man swallowed noisily. 'I have a confession to make,' he said after a slight pause. 'I'm the man you're lookin' for.'

'That's why you're here. That young fella with me is lookin' to kill the folk who shot his ma and step-pa. I reckon he'll deal with Smith outa town. Then he'll come gunnin' for you. I've already sent a telegraph message to Fort Lincoln. They'll be sendin' for you any time now. I'll stay in the jailhouse until they arrive.'

'You'll let my wife know what's happened?'

'I reckon the mayor will take care of that. He's a man who senses a change in wind-direction quicker than most. I figure he's all for law and order right now.'

The marshal rose and picked up the bunch of keys from the desk top. His prisoner followed meekly as he was led to one of the two cells.

'How did you know it was me?' he asked as the door locked on him.

'Well, it was one of your surgical knives that did the job on Ralph

Loman. And that set of knives was brought over to this country late in the war. The importer gave up trying to run the blockade, so only the North got them. They're the sorta things you pick up when you're a federal marshal. Then I saw what a fool I'd been. I'll lay odds you was the doctor what treated that fella who called himself Major Wallace. You found out that he was gettin' a job alongside all that money, and you showed him how to steal it. Too bad it led to murder.'

'That was his doing,' the little man protested. 'I was against anythin' like that. I didn't want killings.'

'Well, it's sure led to quite a few more. And I'd guess you wasn't deliverin' babies the night that freight-haulin' fella got killed. I'll bet you was right here in town and gave Larry Smith his orders. I shoulda realized sooner. Ralph Loman was scared to hell, but he'd open the door to you. The one person he trusted was his doctor.'

'You're quite right, Marshal. That's

how it all happened.'

Hank Donovan went back to the desk and placed the keys in a drawer. He crossed to the stove, poked the dwindling embers, and added some more wood. He made some coffee for himself and his prisoner and the two sat drinking it in almost comradely fashion for a while. Then, as the marshal went over for a refill and lifted the coffee-pot, the door of the jailhouse flew open and Larry Smith was framed against the light.

The federal man had no time to make a move. Smith took in the situation and drew his gun. The coffee-pot hit the floor amid a spray of hot liquid as Hank Donovan went for his own Colt. It was only half-out of the holster when Larry Smith opened fire.

The shot took the federal man in the upper chest. He reeled back against the desk and his eyes went blank as he collapsed on the floor.

Larry Smith took out the cell keys and released the doctor.

'I'm quittin' town, Doc,' he snarled, 'and we got no time for talkin' all polite. We're goin' to your house and you're handin' over every red cent you and that wife of yours have got left. And all her jewellery. So just walk peaceable down the street and neither of you get hurt.'

The marshal looked in one of the desk drawers, found the cash-box and emptied the contents into his pocket. He ushered the little man out of the door and pushed through the crowd that was gathering.

'Step aside, folks,' he ordered. 'We got trouble. A fella back there was tryin' to take over the town. The doc and me is sortin' things out. So just don't get yourselves involved.'

The crowd parted for their lawman while the mayor watched uneasily from a distance. Nobody noticed the arrival of Bill Danvers until his horse pushed its way towards Larry Smith. Doc Mason saw his chance.

'He's just shot the federal marshal!'

he shouted desperately. 'Mr Donovan's hurt bad in the jailhouse back there!'

Larry Smith had been facing in the opposite direction but now turned to see the man on horseback coming through the crowd. He pushed the doctor away, and the man stumbled against a hitching-rail before falling to his knees. Support for the lawman suddenly deserted the crowd and there was a murmur of anger as one woman ran to help the popular medico to his feet.

'You keep outa this, fella!' the town marshal yelled at the newcomer. 'I'm takin' no lip from a snot-nosed kid like you.'

Bill Danvers dismounted and somebody took the rein from him. The lawman found himself facing a young man whose hand was already hovering near the gun at his side.

'I'm gonna kill you,' Bill Danvers said quietly. There was something in his voice that scared the marshal.

'I was just doin' my job,' Larry Smith

pleaded. 'I was just takin' orders, fella.'

'And I know who gave them. You'd better draw.'

The crowd suddenly thinned and there was hardly anybody within twenty yards of the two men. They faced each other while the town waited.

It was the lawman who drew first. His hand was trembling, and his thumb slow in finding the hammer. Almost before he had pulled it back, Bill Danvers opened fire. The shot was loud and a dog yelped somewhere close by.

Larry Smith stood for a moment as though he had not been hit. His hand raised the gun and he waved it in the direction of his enemy. But his eyes were glazed and he staggered forward a couple of steps before sinking to the ground. The town marshal was dead.

Bill Danvers looked around the street and then went in to the jailhouse where Doctor Mason was already tending to the injured federal man. Hank Donovan was propped against the cell door, his face pale and blood staining his shirt.

He looked up when Bill entered.

'You seem to have arrived in time, fella,' he wheezed.

'Easy,' the doctor cautioned. He looked up at the newcomer. 'Will you ask Mrs Mason to come over with my bag? I need her help.'

Bill was just about to respond when one of the town lads burst in with the required equipment and a parcel of bandages. The mayor had sent him to the doctor's house and he was now panting as he handed over his burden. Bill Danvers watched as the doctor worked.

'I appreciate this, Doc,' the federal man said quietly. 'It ain't often the fella I'm jailin' is decent enough to tend me.'

'You ain't jailin' him,' Bill Danvers said in a flat voice.

The marshal looked hard at him. 'Don't do anythin' rash, lad,' he cautioned.

'I don't aim to. I'm off now to deal with the one behind all this. I'll leave you to it, Doc.'

Bill Danvers walked down the street and knocked at the door of the doctor's house. Emma Mason opened it and stood aside to let him in. She led the way to the comfortable living-room and picked up the cup of coffee that stood on the table.

'I'd offer you some,' she said, 'if this was a social call. But I reckon it ain't.'

'It ain't, Ma,' Bill said quietly. He looked hard at the neatly dressed woman who stood serenely before him.

'No, I figure as how you're no fool.' She smiled sadly. 'But I never meant for folk to get hurt. That was all the doin' of that Larry Smith. He's been bleedin' us dry ever since my brother was fool enough to use him when that freight-hauler came to town.'

'I'd never figured that Major Wallace was your kin,' Bill admitted with a slight smile.

She nodded. 'Yes. When Tom got wounded at Shiloh, I went to see him at the hospital. He was bad hurt and they'd just told him of this new job with the paymaster. We was dirt-poor, fella. Real dirt-poor. I talked him in to stealin' the cash and showed him how to go about it. But Tom was always hot-headed. Two fellas got killed and that made it a hangin' matter.'

She took another sip of coffee and sat down wearily.

'He posed as a Confederate officer and came south. Then he married that widow woman.'

'My ma.'

She looked surprised. Then smiled. 'So you're a growed-up Bill Danvers. Well, if that don't beat all. I recall you as a kid. Anyway, Tom wrote me to join him out here and Wal Mason arrived at about the same time. I gave him the money to buy out the Yankee doctor who was in Defiance in those days. This town was goin' all Confederate, so we got everythin' he had for sale. Walter was surely one happy man. You shoulda seen his face when he got an eyeful of that surgery back there with all the latest equipment.'

She smiled a little sadly. 'I'd taken quite a shine to him. He's the gentlest soul you could wish to meet and I was proud to accept when he offered marriage.'

'And he didn't know where your money came from?'

'Bless you, no. He thought I was a wealthy widow. He didn't even know that Tom was my brother. Then, after all these years, that freight fella comes to town. Tom put Larry Smith on to him, and then talked too much, I reckon. The next thing, Larry takes over my life. He wants money all the time. I had to tell Walter eventually, but he stood by me. That's the sort of man he is. I suppose he's takin' the blame right now.'

Bill grinned again. 'He is, and Marshal Donovan was all for arrestin' him. Your husband's a good man, Mrs Mason.'

'I sure know it, young fella. What happens now?'

Bill pulled out a chair and sat down opposite her.

'Well, I've done what I came to town to do, and when I speak to Mr Donovan, your husband will be free as air, I hope. I can't answer for what the federal man will do though. Law ain't my sort of thing. I just believe in justice.'

'How did you know I was the one, and not Walter?' the woman asked in a tired voice.

'I checked on his story that he was out deliverin' a baby on the night the freighter fella was killed. So he couldn't have told Larry Smith to do any shooting. And one of the posse I just been ridin' with told me that he was deliverin' another baby when Ralph Loman was killed.'

Mrs Mason brightened up a little. 'Of course he was,' she agreed. 'I should have mentioned that.'

'And that meant that you had to cut Loman's throat.'

She smiled. 'Yes, you're quite right. I was terrified about how much he might know. My brother was such a gabber.

I'd intended Larry Smith to do the job, but the way things were going, I thought it best to do it myself.'

'That's what I figured. A frightened man wouldn't open the door to another fella, but he would to a charitable woman who might take him in a bit of supper. The tray was there by the bed. He didn't get to eat it.'

'I tried to make it look like a suicide. I wasn't very good at it, was I?'

There was an almost skittish smile on her face as she spoke, and Bill Danvers suddenly felt sorry for the woman. He was about to stand up when the door opened and Doctor Mason entered. He looked first at his wife and then at the young visitor.

'You know then?' he asked Bill Danvers.

The young man nodded. 'How's the marshal?' he asked.

'He'll survive, but I'm leavin' him in the jailhouse for now. He mustn't be moved in case the bleedin' starts again. He wants to see you.'

Bill stood up to take his leave and looked from one to the other. The doctor stood behind his wife's chair and rested a hand on her shoulder.

'We won't be runnin' away,' he said quietly.

Hank Donovan was propped up on one of the bunks in the cell nearest the marshal's desk. He was pale but drinking a cup of coffee and holding a conversation with the mayor. The First Citizen took his leave after being assured that the posse was still on the mission for which it had been formed. Bill had given them the route before he followed the deserting marshal. Davy Smith left a happier man although his face clearly showed his curiosity in what the two were going to discuss.

Bill told his story and the federal marshal listened quietly. He gave an occasional grunt or wince as his movements pained him, but for the most part, he bore the injury well.

'So I had the wrong one,' he murmured when the tale was told. 'And it takes a young fella without experience to get the facts right. I sure got a lot to learn. And I figured that case of knives was the prize in the cracker-barrel.'

He laughed silently and shook his head at his own error.

'Well, what do you reckon we do now, young fella?' he asked.

'Go our ways,' Bill suggested. 'I got nothin' against Ma Mason now and I don't reckon as you're anxious to take a woman back for trial.'

'It's sure one hell of a problem. She stole that cash and she killed Ralph Loman. I'm a federal marshal, young fella. I can't forget that, can I?'

He closed his eyes for a moment as though in thought and spoke quietly to nobody in particular.

'I'm gonna be laid up for some time,' he mused, 'and I'm the only lawman in town right now. If Doc Mason and his wife don't wait all patient-like until my people arrive from Fort Lincoln, then they might never be traced. I've solved the case, and I can't do more than that.

Maybe you should go back to their house and tell them both that they're officially under arrest.'

He threw Bill a quizzical look and the young man nodded. He left the jailhouse and went down the street again to the doctor's residence. The mayor was following him at a distance, anxious not to miss anything that was happening in his town.

Mrs Mason was slumped in the wicker-chair and her husband sat weeping in the chair that Bill had previously occupied. The doctor looked up when the young man entered.

'She's dead,' he sobbed. 'She'd put morphine in her coffee. Just to save my reputation. I've lost her.'

Bill Danvers put out a tentative hand and patted him on the shoulder. He left quietly and walked slowly back towards the jailhouse. The mayor caught up with him and reached out a restraining arm.

'Young fella,' he said cheerfully. 'I got somethin' real important to say to you.

You and that federal fella have saved this town. All our troubles is over now and Defiance can settle down again to what it was before all this started. It's a real Southern town where we can hold up our heads and bless the Confederacy for our sense of unity and pride. You got a part to play in all that, young man.'

Bill stopped in his tracks. 'Me, Mr Mayor?'

'Sure. You. We got no marshal now and I reckon as how you'd be the finest marshal that any Southern town could have.'

Bill grinned. 'Mr Mayor,' he said. 'I'd be the last person you'd want as your lawman. I'm a Yankee born and bred.'

THE END

We do hope that you have enjoyed reading this large print book.

Did you know that all of our titles are available for purchase?

We publish a wide range of high quality large print books including:
Romances, Mysteries, Classics
General Fiction
Non Fiction and Westerns

Special interest titles available in large print are:
The Little Oxford Dictionary
Music Book, Song Book
Hymn Book, Service Book

Also available from us courtesy of Oxford University Press:
Young Readers' Dictionary
(large print edition)
Young Readers' Thesaurus
(large print edition)

For further information or a free brochure, please contact us at:
Ulverscroft Large Print Books Ltd.,
The Green, Bradgate Road, Anstey,
Leicester, LE7 7FU, England.
Tel: (00 44) **0116 236 4325**
Fax: (00 44) **0116 234 0205**

THE JAYHAWKERS

Elliot Conway

Luther Kane, one-time captain with Colonel Mosby's raiders, is forced to leave Texas; bounty hunters are tracking down and arresting men who served with the colonel during the Civil War. He joins up with three Missouri brush boys, outlawed by the Union government, and themselves hunted for atrocities committed whilst riding with 'Bloody' Bill Anderson. Now, in a series of bloody shoot-outs, they must take the fight to the red legs to finally end the war against them . . .